TERI POLEN

THE COLONY SERIES : BOOK TWO

THE INSURGENT

Black Rose Writing | Texas

ISBN: 978-1-68433-953-2
PUBLISHED BY BLACK ROSE WRITING
www.blackrosewriting.com

Printed in the United States of America
Suggested Retail Price (SRP) $18.95

The Insurgent is printed in Calluna

*As a planet-friendly publisher, Black Rose Writing does its best to eliminate unnecessary waste to reduce paper usage and energy costs, while never compromising the reading experience. As a result, the final word count vs. page count may not meet common expectations.

For Barbara

THE INSURGENT

I

ELSA

"Hello, Asher."

"Elsa." His voice was coarse and broken, as if it pained him to speak my name.

For ten years he'd assumed I was dead. Now, he was visibly shaken—shimmering eyes wide in shock, trembling hands.

Good. I hoped he fell apart piece by piece until he was nothing more than a pile of disconnected body parts.

A broad smile lit up Silas's face. He was positively gleeful. "I'll give the two of you some privacy. No doubt you have family matters to discuss. So much to catch up on." He stopped beside me and gently kissed my forehead. "We'll speak later," he murmured, and then exited the room, softly closing the door behind him.

Ash's face flashed with confusion. "How are you here?"

"So, you do remember me. And that you had sisters."

His hand quivered as he lifted it toward my face. "You're... alive."

I slapped his hand away. He jerked it back as if he'd been burned. What right did he have to touch me? To even be in the same room with me? "Don't act so surprised, Asher. Yes, I'm alive, but you had nothing to do with it," I sneered. Not an attractive expression, but I couldn't help myself. "You never came back for us."

He shook his head. "No. No. That's not true. I came back later that day with Patrick and his family after the soldiers were gone. We all searched for you and Cami for hours. Days."

I shrugged. "Whatever. Soldiers took Cami and me back to the Colony. They found the hiding spot where you stashed us just before sunset." I narrowed my eyes, accusing him. Condemning him. "You made a promise, and we trusted you." Even after all these years, no matter how hard I tried to put it behind me, the ache still hovered just below the surface. Asher had abandoned us. When I was a child, my big brother had been the sun and the moon to me, someone I trusted to always be there. And he'd left us to rot.

Pain shot across his face, and he staggered back a step. I wanted to hurt him. Wanted him to suffer endlessly, to feel everything I'd felt after he'd chosen to leave his two defenseless sisters behind and save himself. To experience the agony of being torn from Cami's side, my arms reaching for her as I screamed her name.

"What happened to Cami?" he asked quietly, voice shaking.

I gritted my teeth. "She didn't survive. The last time I saw her, she was being carried to a harvest center. She didn't go willingly." The dull ache that usually accompanied thoughts of Cami now erupted into a piercing pain in my chest and I winced. Sometimes late at night, I could still hear her telling me to be brave while they took her away. I'd always believed she was more afraid for what would happen to me than her own fate behind the doors of the harvest center.

Asher slumped forward and gripped the back of a chair. Eyes squeezed shut, tears tracked down his face as his shoulders shook with quiet sobs.

"Until the very last minute when the soldiers forced us into the helicopter, she believed you'd come back, too."

Slowly straightening, he wiped his face with his sleeve, walked around the chair, then collapsed into it. "Elsa, I never wanted to leave the two of you, but I was following Dad's plan. So was Cami. You were too young to understand—"

"Don't patronize me! I understood just fine," I snapped. "*Your* life continued. *You* just substituted one family for another when you went to live with Patrick and Anna. And I hear you're with Brynn?" I crinkled my nose. "Kind of disturbing, her being like your sister, don't you think? Considering your track record with sisters, I don't expect it to last."

He winced as if I'd slapped him. "Elsa, please. Not a day went by that I didn't think of you and Cami and wonder what happened to you. I thought you were both dead, and I mourned you for years! You have no idea what it's been like for me, everything I've been through."

"What you've been through? What *you've* been through?" Unbelievable. The nerve of him. My hands trembled. "You selfish bastard! Don't you get it? Because you left us, Cami died! I was a child, an orphan who had no one." I remembered the fear I'd felt after Cami was gone, wondering what would happen to me. Who would take care of me. If they didn't kill me first. "Don't you want to know how I survived? How I'm able to stand here in front of you?"

Ash was quiet a long moment as he stared at me. Evaluated me. I could imagine the types of sordid scenes that played in his head. "Yes I want to know, but after what I just witnessed between you and Reeves, I'm almost afraid to hear it."

He used Silas's name in a careless, disrespectful way. That tone would change when he became A36. I raised my chin and looked down at him, his body still slumped in the chair. "That's Director Reeves to you. Silas saved me from the harvest center. He saw something in me, gave me a home, and put me through training. Thanks to a generous gift of new genes, I'm not that clumsy little girl who trailed behind you anymore. I'm now his most valuable operative."

Asher launched himself out of the chair and advanced in my direction, his acrimony propelling him across the floor. He came to a stop only inches away, towering over me, but I refused to cower in fear. Even nearly fully grown, I didn't reach his shoulders.

"Gave you a home? How can you work for the man responsible for the deaths of our sister and parents? Who's killed thousands of other innocent people? Someone suffered and died to give you those genes. Someone like Cami." His eyes flashed in rage, hands clenching and unclenching. Every instinct told me to run, to put distance between us. But I stood my ground. If I showed any sort of weakness, he'd use it against me. Maybe not now, but he'd file it away for future use. "And what about the things he's done to me? To Brynn and Anna? Do you even know what I am? Reeves is everything our parents tried to protect us from. Why we were in hiding all those years. He's a monster, Elsa!"

Anger exploded from his body, and I could almost feel its tentacles wrap around me and squeeze. I knew what he was. What they'd created him to be. I'd seen the footage from the attack on the Insurgent compound, the way he'd ripped through soldiers and tossed them aside like broken toys. It was terrifying. *He* was terrifying.

"I know exactly what and who you are. Now you'll have the chance to show everyone what you can do instead of wasting your talents rescuing hostages," I retorted. "Do you have any idea the problems you've caused for the Colony? Interrupting the supply flow? Causing the loss of enormous amounts of product?"

Asher gaped at me in disbelief, like I'd suddenly sprouted horns and a tail. "H-how can you even say that? Elsa, he murdered our family. Don't you understand? How can you honestly believe what you're doing is right? You know what our parents went through to safeguard us from him and this place. Silas isn't your family. *I* am. I'm all you have left."

"*My* father was slain because he took something that didn't belong to him. *My* mother was killed because neither of them would give up information about you. They both died protecting *you*, Ash, so maybe you should rethink who's actually responsible for their deaths!"

The blood drained from his face, leaving his skin the color of spoiled milk. I hoped his guilt left a gaping wound in his heart that never healed or gave him a peaceful night for the rest of his days. It was the least he deserved.

"And as for us being family? We never were. You're not my brother. We're not blood relatives. You were only there because my father took pity on you and stole you from the lab where you were manufactured." He staggered backward and fell into the chair as if his bones had turned to liquid. "Silas is my only family. You're nothing to me."

•　　•　　•　　•

"So, was the joyous family reunion all that you'd hoped?" Silas lounged in his favorite chair by the fireplace in his quarters, a glass of brandy on the end table beside him. At the second highest level of the twenty-story Tower, his residence was one floor below his office. He could have lived anywhere else in the Colony, had a home with lush gardens or stunning water views, but had always preferred to reside in the Tower where he could be close to his work. After he'd taken me in, I'd lived here with him. He'd given me everything I could have asked for, and I'd never wanted for anything. But those were material things. What I'd wanted was time with him, just the two of us. A real father/daughter relationship, since I remembered little of my biological father.

I dropped into the seat across from him, enjoying the warmth of the fire. "Depends on who you ask. I suspect Asher hoped for a different outcome. I only wish I could have gouged his wound deeper."

Silas crossed his legs and quirked a brow. "You'd have preferred tears and groveling at your feet while he pled for forgiveness? Or are you referring to wounds that draw blood?"

I grinned. "I wanted to gut him and watch his eyes dim as the life bled out of him. But either would have given me pleasure."

Silas grinned in a teasing manner. "Elsa, now that I've finally acquired A36, I can't have you injuring him." He lifted the glass of brandy and took a sip. "Not that you could even if you tried. Nothing life-threatening, anyway. Your father stole him when he was barely two years old. Because of Garrett, I've waited almost sixteen years to utilize my perfect soldier. And I've got big plans for him."

"Care to let me in on those plans? You know you can count on me to help out in any way I can."

He reached over and patted my hand. "Of course, my dear, but you're far too valuable to me where you are. I trust only three people in the world, and two of them are sitting in this room. Once A36 is ready for the field, we'll discuss how your talents can better assist the Colony. Perhaps the two of you could become partners. Just think of what you could accomplish together."

I balked at his suggestion. "You know I prefer to work alone. And I get the impression A36 isn't much of a team player. Besides, I don't trust him. From what I've seen, he's too volatile. Who's to say he wouldn't snap my neck if I looked at him cross-eyed? Remember what he did to Everly."

Silas huffed out a breath in disgust. "Frankly, I'm surprised he waited so long to kill her. That woman was useless. A36 did me a favor."

The fire popped, and the lazy flickering of flames nearly hypnotized me as I pondered Silas's words. It was a mistake to put his faith in A36 so quickly. No matter what Silas said, I'd never be comfortable working with him. It would be impossible to let my guard down. "I'd still be careful about trusting him. We don't know where his loyalties lie as A36. Asher is easy to control. A36? Not so much. He's a wild card."

Silas emptied his glass, rose from the chair, then kissed the top of my head. "'You're wise beyond your years. Don't worry. It's taken care of. You leave tomorrow?"

"Yes. I'll be out for the next few days."

"Be safe."

I grinned. "I always am."

2

ASHER

Three Months Later

I'd been lonely for twelve weeks. My only interactions had been with my trainer, who only spoke to me when necessary, and the meal delivery person who never uttered a word. No quips about the weather, mentions of kids or spouses, or a family pet. Not even a spiteful comment about me finally being locked up. My regimen was quite boring, incredibly repetitive, and rigidly driven by an unrelenting clock.

Sleep—very little.

Train—almost every waking moment.

Eat—purely for energy.

Silas wanted me in prime physical condition before he sent me out into the world to become his demon assassin. I grudgingly admitted to being in the best shape of my life. Between the high protein meals and long training sessions, I'd gained twenty pounds of muscle.

Like the fatted calf before the slaughter, my days were numbered.

I hadn't even seen Silas. Not that I was complaining. I figured this period was the calm before the storm, and I welcomed any reprieve from being in his presence. It gave me the opportunity to daydream about all the creatively painful ways I'd kill him.

Today, my time was up. Silas had summoned me to his office. My best guess was that it was time I went to work.

Truth be told, I was grateful he'd given me three months to myself after my dumpster fire of a reunion with Elsa. I'd still been reeling from the loss of Brynn, Anna, and Noah less than an hour earlier. The shock of seeing her standing before me, the adoring little sister I'd thought lost all those years ago, was like a ray of sunshine piercing through an unrelenting storm at sea. Which had quickly turned into a dagger stabbing my heart. The brief hope I'd harbored of us being a family again was annihilated by her venomous words of hatred.

She'd been here inside the Colony all those years. All the months Brynn and I were held captive, Elsa walked these corridors and followed Silas's orders. She'd known I was in this building and never visited me. The brother she hadn't seen in a decade. The callous young woman who'd shattered my hopes, who considered Silas a father, bore no resemblance to the little sister I remembered. Our parents would be mortified at what she'd become.

I sighed heavily. At what I would soon become.

Mom and Dad had done everything in their power to hide us from Silas. They'd relocated us to a secluded house in the country, disguised the three of us on the rare occasion we were in public, taught me to hide my abilities, and continuously drilled us on escape plans. We'd learned how to survive if we had to run and instructed in ways to stay off the grid. In the end, all their efforts were for nothing. Cami died in captivity, Elsa was raised by the devil they'd hidden us from, and both of us worked for him in his dark hell of a utopian kingdom.

I'd never be able to convince her I hadn't abandoned her and Cami. We'd searched for days after they went missing and asked other Insurgent sectors to notify us if they were spotted or located. Patrick and Anna had comforted me countless nights as I sobbed inconsolably over the loss of my family, blaming myself for the presumed deaths of my sisters.

Elsa denied we were family and disowned me as a brother. Insisted we didn't share parents and claimed Silas as her family now. That sickened me to my core. Knowing he raised her, accepting she willingly resided under the roof of the man who'd made us orphans and was responsible for the death of our sister was like a cancer deep inside me that threatened to metastasize the longer Elsa stayed here.

Here I was at the mercy of Silas. Forced to kick puppies and dismember children for all I knew. Permanently separated from my family if I wanted them to live. A smirk tugged at the corner of my mouth as I thought about what Brynn would say. "Quit feeling sorry for yourself, Princess. Suck it up and make a plan. *Fight*, Ash." I'd cling to that notion as long as I was able.

Two guards arrived to accompany me to Silas's office. I held my hands in front of me and allowed them to cuff me. Disarming them and escaping would have been effortless. I wouldn't have broken a sweat. But the knowledge that my actions had deadly repercussions was a constant black cloud hovering over me. Disobeying equaled death for my loved ones. So, I followed them like an obedient child through long corridors while people stopped to gawk in my direction and turned to whisper at each other excitedly. Or in fear. Maybe some of them had witnessed my failed attempt at rescuing Brynn on the day I'd believed she'd died in my arms from a sniper bullet to the chest. Maybe they'd also seen me systematically slay the many guards who'd entered her room.

Whatever the case, no one was curious enough or stupid enough to get too close. And that was fine by me.

Elevator doors opened to the lobby outside Silas's office. The guards followed behind me as I exited, then stumbled into me as I stopped abruptly. Directly in front of me sat a familiar woman behind a desk who met my gaze.

Paige.

I blinked. No, that was ridiculous. If Paige sat here quietly, it was only because she'd killed the previous occupant and stashed the body underneath the desk. I tilted my head to the side. Closer examination revealed the cheek bones weren't quite as defined and her eyes not the brilliant green I remembered. Still, the resemblance was unsettling. Uncanny.

Several years ago, Paige walked into our Insurgent sector seemingly out of nowhere and asked to join us. Like Noah, Brynn, and me, she was trained at a young age and a quick learner. I counted myself lucky she'd requested placement on my team the day I'd been named leader. She'd always had my back, always watched out for her fellow team members, and was deadly and accurate in the field, but I didn't know much more about her now than the day she'd arrived at our compound. Paige was an intensely private person, and I respected that. A friend and one of the few people I trusted in this world, she'd witnessed my transformation to A36 for the first time. Instead of fleeing in fear, she'd stuck by me. Although I'd still been in control, other Insurgents who'd known me for years cowered and kept their distance after watching the brutal ways I'd slaughtered several Colony soldiers.

If it had really been her sitting in front of me now, I imagined how the scenario might play out. Guards swiftly disarmed, rapid gunfire, bodies dropping. We'd be far outnumbered, but the two of us would go down fighting and cause some serious damage before being restrained. Maybe even barricade ourselves inside Silas's office and end him before more guards arrived.

I sighed heavily. It was a pleasant fantasy. Definitely the best part of my day.

The woman's gaze moved over my body, pausing at places I'd most likely hide a weapon. The guards had searched me before I left my room, but she was cautious and efficient. I admired that.

When she'd finished scanning me, she assessed me with a look that made me feel like something that needed to be scraped off her shoe. "A36."

My fists clenched involuntarily. "No, I'm Asher," I said through gritted teeth.

She raised a brow as her lips curved into a smile. "Not for long. Director Reeves is waiting for you."

I squared my jaw, then turned toward the double doors on my right. Knots tightened in my stomach at the thought of what would happen behind them. Over the past three months, I'd devised plan after plan of escape then discarded them in frustration. There was nothing I could do. Silas had me backed into a corner, and if I made any attempt to fight my way out, Brynn, Noah, and Anna would die. End of story.

Glancing at the sitting area to the right outside the office, I noted a few people waiting. I halted. Colonel Ackerman stared back at me. Along with Silas, I assumed he'd also celebrated my imprisonment, and I expected a smug look of victory and satisfaction on his face. Maybe a delighted or even taunting expression. But unless I was wrong—and I prided myself on being able to read people—his eyes were rounded in fear, his face ashen. He looked ready to bolt at any second. Was I misreading him? If anything, he held all the power and had no reason to be afraid of me. As for how I felt about him? If feelings of hatred were fatal, he'd be struck dead before he took his next breath.

I closed my eyes and inhaled deeply as the guards opened the door to Silas's office. Years of ingrained training took over, and I immediately examined my surroundings. Corner room. Soaring skylights. Inky marble tiles. Glass desk directly ahead of me, with two gray leather chairs in front of it. Floor-to-ceiling windows behind it, as well as on my left, where a large, rectangular conference table sat. A massive, gray stone wall flanked my right. I searched for any other exits—none—and the presence of any physical threats or weapons—also none, unless I counted the guards who'd followed me in. But I didn't.

Silas sat behind the desk, wearing the smug look of victory and satisfaction I'd expected from Ackerman. He watched me closely and evaluated my every move as if I was something he was considering purchasing. But he already owned me. He knew it. I knew it.

Behind him and to the left, Declan leaned casually against a bookshelf, his legs crossed at the ankles. He met my gaze without hesitation, brow furrowed as if trying to solve a puzzle.

This I hadn't expected.

The night I'd mistakenly believed I was finally fleeing the Colony with my family, Anna told me to trust Declan, so I had. He'd disguised me as a corpse by loading me on a gurney and covering me with a sheet, then wheeled me to the morgue, close to the hallway where I was to escape with Anna and Brynn.

Yet here he stood at Silas's side. Literally his right-hand man.

I glared at him in question, and he very subtly shook his head. I assumed it was a signal not to give him away. Had helping us just been a ploy? Did his loyalty truly lie with the Colony? He'd known Anna's escape plan and could easily have ratted us out to Silas. Maybe Declan was the reason I'd been detained. I clenched my jaw and reconsidered my decision to let him live after we'd been thrown into the training ring together as Everly goaded me from the sidelines, demanding I kill him.

I directed my attention back to Silas. He still had that reptilian air about him, as if he was coiled and ready to strike at any moment. I had the feeling he'd consume my soul if I allowed him in.

He gestured to a chair in front of the desk, and I slowly lowered myself into it. I was surprised when one of the soldiers removed my wrist restraints before joining the other at the doors behind me. I'd half expected to be hogtied when in Silas's presence.

"You're looking very fit, A36. I trust you've been taking advantage of our accommodations and amenities?"

Accommodations and amenities? Was he serious? This was no luxury resort that catered to my every whim, and his fake pleasantries were wasted on me. I wasn't in the mood to play along with his games. "Let's just skip the crap and get to the part where you tell me why I'm here."

He raised his chin indignantly. "There's no reason to be impolite. Working relationships are built on mutual respect and require a certain level of civility, wouldn't you agree, Declan?"

"Absolutely, sir."

My suspicions were confirmed. Declan was bought and paid for. He'd persuaded Anna to trust him so he'd be privy to the escape plan, then used that information to slither his way up the ladder to the top of the food chain. Giving up the location of our compound was strike one. Deceiving Anna was strike two. A third wouldn't be offered. We were done.

With nothing to say to either one of them, I sat in stony silence. Check that. I had a long string of profanities chomping at the bit to be released, but nothing would be gained except my short-term satisfaction. Brynn might pay for my outburst, and I'd still be sitting here before Silas when it was all over. Unlike Declan, I'd never bow to him.

But I could pretend.

I'd be that chess pawn he wanted. Follow his instructions. Make him think he could trust me. Maybe he'd grow too comfortable around me and let down his guard with safety precautions the way Everly did. Snapping her neck had taken only a second. I exhaled loudly, still regretting it hadn't been more painful.

Silas sighed heavily when it was evident I wouldn't participate in polite conversation. "I have big plans for you, A36. Monumental things are happening here at the Colony, and you'll play an integral part. In fact, until we finally brought you home, I didn't think we'd be able to proceed with these plans." His eyes sparkled with excitement.

If this new project made him that happy, it was guaranteed to hurt plenty of other people. And I wanted no part of it.

"This is your chance to be a part of something historical, A36. Aren't you curious to know what it is?"

He stared at me like he was waiting for a genuine answer.

"Curious? That's not the word I'd use. I don't think you really want to know how I'm feeling right now, Silas. But I'd enjoy showing you." A devilish grin split my face as I cracked my knuckles.

Fear flashed in his eyes as they darted to my hands before his face assumed its usual mask of steely confidence. He met my gaze again. "The Colony is expanding." Expanding? Silas using that word was ominous at best and terrifying at worst. "One of our small neighboring territories, Eglan, is quite interested in our way of life and plans to offer genetic alterations to its more deserving citizens. Now that you're here, I'm confident we'll have the support needed to assist in implementing the changes."

Terror knotted my gut, but I refused to show it. "What does this have to do with me?"

Silas waved a hand in Declan's direction. Declan opened his data pad, then cleared his throat. "A36 will ensure cooperation of the chosen donors when being gathered for transport to the harvest centers. He'll use any means necessary to eliminate all obstacles that interfere with transportation. At the harvest..."

My breathing ceased as the meaning of Declan's words descended on me. They wanted me to hurt parents trying to protect their children. Harm children and adults fighting to free themselves. "No," I interrupted. "Absolutely not. I won't do it."

Silas's face hardened, and his eyes bored into mine. "You will do anything I demand. Don't pretend you have a choice."

I bolted out of my seat and slammed my fists on his desk, towering over him as he flinched and sank back in his chair.

Declan pulled a gun from inside his jacket and trained it on me. The guards behind me lunged in my direction, but Silas held up a hand to halt them.

"I'm an Insurgent. I rescue innocents from harvest centers, not deliver them to their deaths. I *will not* have any part in this project and promise to do everything in my power to ensure it doesn't happen."

Silas signaled for Declan and the guards to stand down, then rose from his chair and drew himself up. He looked at me with a surety in his face that he would not be questioned. "You are no longer an Insurgent. You're an assassin or anything else I need you to be." His voice was frosty with a sharp edge. "You don't question my orders. Your job is to execute them quickly and efficiently. *This* is what you were created to be. The life you lived outside this facility was never yours. *This* is your life now."

I leaned over and braced my hands on his desk, meeting his gaze with steely determination. "No."

"Declan, please inform A36 what happens when he disobeys orders," he said, his stare still locked with mine.

"Soldiers will immediately be deployed to kill your family. With the trackers embedded in Brynn and Anna, we know their locations at any given time. Noah will most likely be with them or close by and will also be eliminated."

His words pierced my chest like the icy blade of a dagger. Visions of my family's bullet-ridden bodies flashed in my mind. The excruciating pain and emptiness I'd felt when I'd believed Brynn dead wrapped its icy fingers around me and squeezed. I closed my eyes and crumpled back into the chair, defeated. He had me. I'd known this, of course, but the horror of the heinous acts he wanted me to commit had temporarily overshadowed that surety. Running my hands through my hair, I grasped at some futile attempt to avoid doing this. Anything. I was desperate.

"I've been given a preliminary list of donors to acquire, with their locations, ages, and descriptions noted. You will personally oversee their acquisitions and ensure there is no loss of donors. You'll receive a final list, but Declan has a preliminary copy for you to look over."

Scanning that list was the absolute last thing I wanted to do. The longer I avoided it, the more time I could give to the targets out there who had no idea what the future had in store for them. I kept my eyes downcast and made no move to accept it.

"Take. The. List." Silas left no room for discussion. I knew the repercussions if I refused.

I ripped my gaze from the floor and glared in Declan's direction. He repulsed me, and I hoped he felt how much I wanted to reach down his throat and rip out every internal organ from his body right now. I needed to lash out at someone, and he was an easy target. Judging by the way his hand trembled as he passed me his pad, he felt those vibes loud and clear.

Horror and disbelief settled in my gut as I swiped through the list. Over fifty percent of those listed were children below the age of ten. Young children who had barely started their lives. "What the hell is this, Silas? These are kids."

He raised a brow. "Using children as donors isn't a new concept. Is there a problem?"

I stared at him in shock. Was he serious? "A problem? Harvesting genes from anyone against their will is unconscionable, yet you still do it. Killing children for something as simple as their eye color is monstrous and immoral."

A satisfied grin slid across his face. "Since that's exactly what you'll be doing, you've just described yourself, A36."

3

ASHER

I slammed the door behind me, the force cracking the frame. Inhaling deeply, I tried to squash the urge to rip it from its hinges. My gaze swept over the clean, straight lines and hard angles of my room. Perfectly and tastefully decorated in shades of white and gray. Perfect like the residents of the Colony, their houses, and places of business. Even the parks resembled an unblemished, lush paradise. Adrenaline and rage careened through my veins and begged for an outlet, yearning for release.

I didn't want perfection. I wanted my own life. My family.

Brynn.

What Silas demanded of me was unfathomable. I could never commit such abominable acts. Rounding up innocent people and transporting them to certain death at harvest centers? Even children? Tearing them away from their mothers and fathers? He expected me to use physical force to prevent those parents from fighting for their kids. To kill them if necessary.

My heart sank at the thought of the Colony expanding. There weren't enough Insurgents to keep people out of harvest centers in our own area. How could we expect to save citizens in other territories? The thought of those leaders even entertaining the idea of adopting this way of life, let alone approving and welcoming it, made my stomach roil. What the hell was wrong with them? Where was their moral compass?

The world would be a better place if we stripped the genes of Silas and the other leaders and destroyed them so their DNA would never again pollute the gene pool of our society. No one would have to ask me to round them up. I'd gladly do it. Using any means necessary to ensure they made it to the harvest center? No problem. Got it covered.

But then I'd just have to wipe out any of their descendants. Maybe they were innocent. Maybe not. The thought that Silas had reproduced and had some sort of demon spawn walking around was enough to give me nightmares. To my knowledge, he had no children. That was one reason to rejoice.

It didn't matter how much Silas's demands went against everything I believed in and fought for. My hands were tied. Follow his orders or my family would die. I knew without a doubt Brynn would say to sacrifice her, Anna, and Noah. What were three lives compared to so many others? If I did, Silas would have nothing left to hold me here. I'd be out from under his thumb. From a logical perspective, taking my personal interest out of the equation and leaving their fate in his hands was the right decision. The rational choice.

But I couldn't bring myself to condemn them to their deaths. The mother who'd raised me as her own, my best friend and brother, and the woman who loved me fiercely, the one I'd given my heart to when we were only children. I wasn't strong enough. I couldn't do it.

And Elsa.

When I'd learned she was here and stood before me safe and alive, a vision flashed in my mind. The two of us would fight together to be free of this place, find our way back to the Insurgents, and destroy Silas and the Colony. We'd have a happily ever after and become a family.

It was a simple dream that now seemed like an impossibility.

But that was before she'd taken an axe and cleaved into my chest cavity, torn my heart free and shredded it after saying I wasn't her brother. Wasn't her family. A metaphorical axe maybe, but it sure felt real. She wouldn't be tossing any lifelines in my direction.

During my months here, I'd concluded Silas had brainwashed my sister and infected her with his lies because he couldn't have A36. It was my punishment for not being here. For daring to use my abilities, the abilities Silas had bestowed upon me, to rescue hostages instead of killing for him.

Somehow, he'd predicted all those years ago this day would come. And he'd make me pay.

Anger and frustration pulsed through me. I drew back my fist and punched the wall, leaving a hole the size of a watermelon. I'd tried to reason with Elsa, make her understand what happened that day, but the girl I'd known, the clumsy little sister who'd followed me nearly everywhere, was gone. In the past three months I'd been here, she hadn't visited at all and made no effort to contact me—not that I'd expected her to. She'd made it crystal clear she didn't want me in her life.

I had nothing.

Brynn, Noah, and Anna only stayed alive if I followed orders. Elsa hated me. Even Declan, a last pathetic, desperate hope, had abandoned me and aligned himself with Silas.

I was alone.

At Silas's mercy.

My vision flashed red. I roared in frustration, then tore through the room. I snatched drawers from chests and smashed them against the smooth white walls, marring them with holes and cracks. Wood shards sprayed my face. I spun around to the bed. The mattress offered no resistance when I punched through it and ripped out springs and cushioning. Roundhouse kicks decimated the closet doors and left splintered remains on the floor.

I imagined Silas's face on the receiving end of every blow I landed.

Chest heaving from exertion and rage, my lips curved into a half smile at the results of my destruction. What was immaculate and unblemished moments ago was now nothing more than a pile of rubbish.

And none of it helped.

Frustration and injustice surged from deep within me, ripped through my chest and erupted as a prolonged scream that left me hoarse. I was certain somewhere in this prison Silas heard me, triumphant at finally getting what he'd wanted for over a decade.

He had me. He had A36.

Knowing he could harm my family at any moment if I refused him anything—or just because he damn well felt like it—had forced me into a three-sided iron box. My only move was to step onto the path he'd laid before me. A path filled with death and destruction that would tear me apart piece by piece and condemn my soul to hell for eternity.

Nearly eighteen years ago, I was built in a lab and genetically engineered to be the perfect assassin. To follow orders without question. Kill without emotion. I was physically stronger than anyone in the Colony, could outmaneuver and out-strategize nearly any opponent. I could end an enemy's life in the span of a heartbeat.

All of that and yet, I was helpless. My life wasn't my own anymore. Maybe it never would be again.

I ran my hands through my sandy locks. My hair was down to my shoulders now—satisfying to grip in frustration as I paced my windowless room, the pent-up energy leaving me no other option. If I stilled, I'd implode. Maybe that wasn't such a bad thing.

Angry tears brimmed my eyes. It wasn't fair. After years of believing Anna died in battle along with her husband, Patrick, we'd just gotten her back. Noah had assumed the position of Controller soon after his father's death and blamed himself for the destruction of our compound. Disappointing Patrick was his greatest fear. And I couldn't be there to help him.

Brynn, my beginning and my end. I had to accept that I'd never be with her again. Never trail my finger down her crooked nose that she hated, or wake curled around her warm body. She'd grieve for me. Undoubtedly try to find me, but Silas would put a stop to that. Maybe she'd eventually forget about me and move on with her life. Love someone else. I wanted her to be happy, but the thought of her with another man stole the breath from my lungs and the strength from my limbs.

My last image of her, the picture that haunted my dreams, was when I thought she'd died. I held her in my arms and watched the life drain from her eyes as blood seeped through her shirt from the wound in her chest.

Anna told me her daughter had survived. I believed her, of course, but I'd hoped my last image of Brynn would be better. Something happier I could hold onto. I hadn't even been able to tell her goodbye. And I lost a little more of myself every day we were apart.

I dropped my head in my hands and squeezed my eyes shut. Too much. Everything was too much. The misery, disappointment, helplessness. It weighed on me like a ten-ton boulder and threatened to crush me—I couldn't bear it. Silas had ordered me to kill. I'd slaughter any soldiers that stood in my way. But children? Parents fighting to save them? I imagined those tiny, confused faces staring back at me in terror, kids who didn't understand why they had to die. I could never be the cold and callous assassin Silas demanded.

The memory of what I'd done to those Colony soldiers when they'd attacked our compound played through my mind—the way I'd slashed, disemboweled, and shot my way through anyone that stood between me and Brynn. I'd done what was required to try and save both her and our compound. But it wasn't just me doing the killing. A36 had made his macabre debut that night and shown me what I'd truly been capable of.

What I'd been created for.

Something washed over me like the wave of an ocean, and I felt it ripple through my body. I gasped and struggled to pull air into my lungs. Had all the oxygen been sucked from the room? My chest felt heavy from the exertion of trying to breathe. Dark spots clouded my vision and I stumbled as the room spun.

I hurt. Everything hurt from the roots of my hair down to the tips of my toes. My heart galloped, and a sharp pain stabbed deep inside my head. Maybe I was dying. At least I'd be released from Silas's unyielding grasp. He'd warned me what would happen if I tried to end my life. What if I died, but not by my own hand? Maybe my body was willing itself to let go.

My legs collapsed, and I fell to my knees. The throbbing in my head hammered against my skull. Like my brain was trying to force its way out somehow. It was agonizing, and my stomach twisted with nausea. My lungs heaved, still short of oxygen. I crawled over to what was left of the mattress and rolled onto it.

I'm here.

Clutching my head, I searched the room for the source of the voice. I still couldn't see. Someone could have easily slipped in while I destroyed the room.

Give me control.

So close. It was so close. But where?

End your pain.

In my head. The voice echoed in my head.

It was him. A36.

Through the crushing agony I gritted my teeth and struggled to force the word through my lips.

"No."

But I felt him clawing his way out, inch by inch from the deep abyss inside me where I'd kept him imprisoned for my own sanity and the safety of others.

You have nothing left.

I squeezed my eyes shut and shook my head. But he spoke the truth. All that held me together were the scars of everything I'd lost. Everyone I'd ever loved.

And scars could be easily ripped open.

I'm here. Use me.

It would be simple. So effortless to surrender to him. Like falling asleep. Let A36 do Silas's bidding. He could handle it. No feelings. No guilt. It was just business.

I could disappear into myself and remember better times.

Be with her again.

With my family.

So easy.

Exactly.

I gave A36 what he desired. Eyes closed, I held onto the vision of Brynn's face, the smile she reserved only for me, and the pain faded away.

Floating in the darkness, my burdens lifted. Air filled my lungs as I inhaled deeply.

Only one thing tethered me to the present, one last link. The whisper of a voice I longed to hear.

Remember who you are.

But it was so far away. Out of my reach.

And I let go.

4

DECLAN

The young girl was terrified, eyes wide, hands trembling. Fear had stolen her voice, and silent tears slid down her tiny face as a white-coated man led her into the harvest room. After soldiers killed her parents for fighting back when they'd stolen her away, there was no one left to come for her. Death was only minutes away.

She'd heard of Insurgents, a rebel group who rescued hostages from harvest facilities, but their numbers had dwindled after an attack on one of their compounds. Since then, even more children had been taken. As she hid behind bushes in her mother's flower garden, she'd witnessed her best friend next door grabbed from her own yard as she'd played, her desperate screams and pleas for help ignored and unanswered by soldiers.

But her hiding place hadn't gone unnoticed, and the Colony soldiers came for her next.

Stumbling into the harvest room, she was greeted with white walls, white floors, and more people wearing white coats who went about their jobs. People who didn't care that a child was being led to her death only steps away from them. Enormous, silver machinery hummed and swished as small lights flashed red, orange, and green. In the center of the room sat the device where she'd meet her end. Only pain and suffering waited for her now. After days spent in the facility with little food and water, no sleep, and no comfort from others, she could only hope death came quickly.

The white-coated man grabbed her by the upper arms then dropped her into a shallow, stainless-steel tub. Icy coldness from the metal seeped through her thin, threadbare gown into her bones. She shivered uncontrollably, either from fear or chills, but probably a combination of the two. Her wrists and ankles were roughly strapped into restraints that secured her to the tub, ensuring no last-minute attempt at escape.

Eyes rimmed with tears, she whispered, "Please."

The man neither acknowledged her nor met her pleading gaze. She was nothing to him but another donor to the Colony. Just a product who served only to supply its wealthy citizens with desirable genetic traits and attributes that catered to their whims. Whatever was trendy that month. In the young girl's case, she had much to offer—perfectly smooth, light brown skin, golden amber eyes, and a cascade of dark curls that tumbled down her back. She'd heard someone mention her eye color was all the rage right now.

Her eyes squinted from the bright overhead lights, then the lid of the device closed over her, encasing her in darkness. She thought this must be what it was like to sleep in a coffin. "Mama?" Her voice quivered.

Vibrations shook beneath her, a rumbling she felt deep in her chest. Even surrounded by darkness, she squeezed her eyes shut. Tears oozed from the corners of her eyes and slid into her hairline. Her fingernails cut into the palms of her hands as she clenched her fists.

Every DNA-containing cell in her body, from the roots of her hair, her internal organs, brain, skin, teeth, and bones, would be extracted from her body. It would be a painful, excruciating death. All that remained would essentially be a pile of mush. From there, the desired DNA would be isolated, precipitation would remove any impurities, and then it would be prepared for implantation into the wealthy recipients who'd purchased it, essentially overwriting their own DNA.

As numerous needles penetrated her tiny body, the young girl's terrified screams went undetected over the clamor of the machinery. Even if they were heard, there was no one left to care...

I shot up in bed, the young girl's piercing screams still echoing in my head. Sweat drenched my body, and my chest heaved as if I'd just run for miles.

The same nightmare had haunted me for months, and I didn't need a therapist to diagnose the underlying cause. Soul-crushing guilt. Because of my own foolish, selfish actions, numerous people, adults and children included, had died at harvest centers.

And I'd betrayed my friends in the worst way possible.

Rubbing my face still damp with tears, I flopped back onto the pillow.

Months ago, while still an Insurgent known as Oz, I'd been captured by the Colony and tortured for information. Insurgents were trained to handle interrogation, but I was on the brink of shaking hands with the grim reaper when I'd been given a choice—a long, drawn out, painful death or a completely new genetic panel in exchange for the location of our compound. And the delivery of Asher Solomon, also known as Subject A36, a Colony-created, genetically enhanced killing machine. No risk there.

As a child, I'd sustained burns over portions of my neck and face after a fire in the house where several other children and I had found shelter. After being captured and taken to a harvest facility, we'd been deemed as possessing undesirable traits, then dumped in the middle of nowhere by Colony soldiers. I'd escaped the fire but failed to save my best friend during all the chaos.

It seemed I had a habit of abandoning my friends.

As an Insurgent, I'd been in love with my field op partner, Paige. She was beautiful, wickedly intelligent, a fierce operative—and far out of my league. We're talking light years. Because I apparently have the mental capacity of a brick, I'd underestimated her and stupidly assumed she didn't want me because of my physical deformities. When Dr. Everly, a scientist who'd helped create A36, offered a new physical package, I'd accepted.

And I'd chosen wrong. So, so wrong.

I'd sold out the friends who had become my only family after losing mine to the Colony.

With my new face and build, I'd infiltrated my former compound for the Colony as Declan, an Insurgent transferring from another sector. I'd worked side-by-side with my friends, even placed on my former team led by Asher. No one had a clue as to my true identity. Using the information I'd given them, Colony soldiers attacked the compound, and many Insurgents lost their lives in the battle. I'd helped capture Brynn, my team member and Asher's longtime girlfriend. If the Colony had her, they controlled Subject A36. Asher swore to kill me the next time we met.

To save Brynn, Asher turned himself in, but releasing her had never been an option. Everly threatened to have her killed if Ash didn't embrace the part of him that was A36 and become the killer he'd been engineered to be. Everly even offered me up as a sacrifice to entice him, but when Asher had the chance to kill me, and believe me, I'd begged him to, he'd spared my life. Said I owed him. Then he'd snapped Everly's neck instead.

I'd paid part of my debt by helping Brynn and her mother, Anna, escape, but the Colony Director, Silas Reeves, had forced Asher to stay by threatening their lives. The role I'd played in their escape was covered up with a clever technical skill I'd learned when I was an Insurgent. I'd framed some other guy who'd never performed a good deed in his life. He was no longer breathing and, in my opinion, the world was a better place without him.

I'm not going to lie. Based on the way I turned the heads of women, and more than a few men, I was pretty drool-worthy. As Oz, I'd been slightly shorter with a wiry, athletic build, and I'd kept my blond hair long enough to partially hide my scars. But now, as Declan? I had the threatening build of a guy you don't want to meet in a dark alley, inky, wavy hair, and turquoise eyes that put provocative smiles on the faces of admirers I passed in the hallways.

And I'd give everything back in a heartbeat if it would repair all the damage I'd caused.

My looks were the result of DNA stripped from the very people I'd protected and rescued as an Insurgent. Most days I couldn't look at myself in the mirror. When Paige revealed her looks were the result of gene stripping, I'd been astonished. As a child, she hadn't been given a choice and was stunned and repulsed when she'd learned what her parents had done. She'd walked away from them and devoted her life to the Insurgents to compensate for their actions.

Her bombshell disintegrated any hopes I'd harbored about us ever being together. Game over, account closed.

So, I'd made a plan. Over the past few months, I'd worked my way up the ladder into Silas's good graces and shaken hands with the devil, all to atone for the wrongs I'd committed. In this case, two wrongs made a right. I was still an Insurgent at heart and had been covertly sending them information and doing everything in my power to help them defeat the Colony. All while overseeing the group of Colony-trained young operatives who were contracted out to other territories.

Their best assassin? Subject C24, Asher's long presumed to be dead younger sister, Elsa. Her enhancements weren't anywhere close to Asher's level, but the girl was vicious at heart and lived to serve Silas.

And Asher? Our meeting in Silas's office was the first time I'd laid eyes on him since he'd been locked away for training. When he'd found me at Silas's side, I'd been terrified Ash would say something about my role in the escape and destroy months of a carefully constructed facade. While he'd been away, I'd tried to think of a logical excuse to get into see him or maybe even bribe my way in, but it wasn't happening. He was locked down tight. I had to gamble that I'd get to him before he saw me with Silas, or he'd keep my secret if I couldn't reach him first.

Judging by the death daggers his eyes hurled in my direction yesterday, there's no doubt he'd reinstated me as number one on his hit list. As far as Ash knew, I was proudly waving the Colony flag. I hoped to intercept him today and convince him everything I did was for the Insurgents, but after I'd threatened his family at Silas's instruction, the chances of him listening to me were nonexistent.

He'd looked utterly destroyed, a broken man when he'd left Silas's office. The demands placed on him were unconscionable, and I honestly didn't know how he'd follow through on them. But I knew he would. Asher would do anything within his power to keep his family safe. And like it or not, his skillset was ideal for what Silas Reeves demanded.

That was another reason connecting with Paige was so crucial. When Asher started working for Silas, he'd put up a ridiculously high body count and wouldn't come away unscathed. Every death would chip away a piece of his soul, and before long he'd be carved into a new shape. The Asher I knew would no longer exist.

Ultimately, that was on me. His destruction would be a product of my betrayal.

Getting him home was part two of my mission. I'd help take down the Colony and get Asher back to his family or die trying. Most days, I felt like my destiny was the latter.

Right now, it was time to get out of bed and shake off another mostly sleepless night, fill my veins with strong coffee, then get to work. I had a performance to prepare for. My meeting with Silas was in an hour.

5

DECLAN

The elevator doors opened into the lavish lobby outside Director Reeves's office. No expense had been spared in decorating his suite. Talk about overindulgence. There was even a statue of Silas in the courtyard fountain at the entrance to the Tower. As Insurgents, we'd mostly relied on generous monetary donations and the kindness of folks outside Colony gates just to keep us fed. Not a lot of money in being a rebel group.

During my time here, the wastefulness of the citizens and the careless way they spent money on ridiculous purchases had stunned me. Hell, Silas's weekly food budget would have kept us and every hostage we rescued fed for months. Their awareness of the world beyond the gates of the Colony was nonexistent.

And I had to pretend to be one of them if I wanted to survive long enough to accomplish my goals.

Jade, Silas's longtime, highly efficient assistant, raised her almond-shaped, emerald green eyes and regarded me as I stepped off the elevator. Her resemblance to Paige was kind of freaky and had nearly rendered me speechless the first time we'd met. That's almost an impossible feat—ask anyone who knows me and has tried unsuccessfully to shut me up. Even the raven-colored hair was the same, although Paige wore hers shoulder length, while Jade's hung straight down her back. If I had to guess, I'd say Jade was somewhere around ten years older. No, I hadn't asked her out.

She'd only distract me, and I couldn't afford to lose focus. But that didn't mean harmless flirting was off the table.

I flashed her my most devastating smile and winked. "Stunning, as usual, Jade."

Which garnered me a stony stare. "He's finishing up with Colonel Ackerman. Have a seat, Declan." She gestured to the leather chairs outside Silas's office, then turned back to her desk, already dismissing me.

The woman was an iceberg. In these weeks since I'd begun meeting regularly with Silas, Jade had never granted me a smile. Not even a twitch of her alluring pink lips. Which I naturally took as a personal challenge. I was determined to earn a smile one of these days.

Nodding in defeat, I tucked my tail and claimed a seat facing the office door. My gaze drifted to the scenery outside as I thought about the message I'd sent Paige a couple days ago. I'd requested a personal meeting with her but remained skeptical she'd even consider it. As Interim Controller, she'd received intel from me for months now, but I'd been funneling it through one of the Insurgents' trusted sources. If it came directly from me, she'd immediately reject it. I needed her to know I was on their side, that I could be valuable to the Insurgents and instrumental in helping take down the Colony. I only hoped she could see past the sins I'd committed against her and the other Insurgents.

Maybe Anna could vouch for me. Sensing my need to redeem myself, she'd asked if I'd help Brynn and her escape, and I'd eagerly agreed. From the first day I'd shown up at the Insurgent compound after losing my family, Anna had always been good to me. In a way, she'd been a surrogate mother to us all. I only hoped she'd be able to sway Paige's decision in my favor.

Shaking my head, I turned my focus back to the meeting with Silas. I needed to be fully present when we met. I swore he possessed an internal divining rod built to sense deception. His soulless black eyes reminded me of a serpent, and I had to force myself to meet his gaze. For months, I'd lived with the fear that he'd discover my betrayal. Which explained why my fingernails were bitten to the quick. It was painful, unattractive, and strongly frowned upon in a place where perfection was everything.

They could take their perfection and shove it—

I nearly jumped as the office doors opened. Colonel Ackerman strode out, glanced in my direction, then gave a curt nod before boarding the elevator. What I wouldn't give to have been in on that meeting. After A36 killed Dr. Everly, Ackerman was moved to another project. As of yet, I hadn't determined exactly what it was. He'd worked closely with Everly for years to locate A36, but I had the distinct impression he hadn't mourned her death. Wouldn't have surprised me if he'd had quite a celebration behind closed doors at being free of that screeching wombat. I'd rejoiced in private for days.

"Declan, you can go in." Jade didn't bother looking up from her task.

Showtime.

As I sauntered into Silas's office, I smirked at the guards posted on either side of the doors. I'd gotten the distinct impression the director enjoyed a little swagger. Brynn always said cockiness oozed from my pores. Might as well put it to use. I'd like to think it was part of the reason I'd advanced so quickly.

Be the person people wanted to see.

Provide the skills they needed.

And then work like hell to keep up the illusion.

One mistake could end not only my life, but my quest to atone for my actions. All my efforts would have been for nothing. I walked a precarious, unforgiving tightrope without a net to catch me if I faltered.

"Come in, Declan. We have much to discuss."

I closed the door behind me, strode across the black onyx marble floor, then sank into the plush gray chair in front of Silas's desk. "Good morning, Director."

His dark gaze bore into me, and I immediately erected a wall around my thoughts. Not that he could read minds. I didn't think so, anyway. If he could, I'd be dead already, but during our first meeting I'd felt a coldness inside, like icy tendrils had penetrated my brain and become privy to my deepest beliefs. Probably just my imagination, but ever since, I'd put up a mental barrier. It was a useless tactic, but it made me feel safer. As safe as I could be in this situation.

Living a lie and selling it to the most dangerous man in the Colony.

Silas rose. He wandered over to the wall of windows that looked out over the expansive city, hands clasped behind his back. Chin raised, he stared down his nose at the streets below. An Emperor surveying his empire.

"I assume you've brought an update of C24's most recent mission?"

"Of course." I opened my data pad and pulled up her debrief. "She returned late last night after successfully terminating her target. During her escape, two extraneous kills were required after she was witnessed leaving the target's room. Housekeeping handled the cleanup."

He nodded. "Excellent."

"Sir, C24 requested a dinner meeting with you this evening. I informed her that on such short notice, you may not be able to accommodate—"

"I'll have Jade clear my schedule," he interrupted. "This assignment lasted longer than expected, and I've missed Elsa's company. Even after moving into her own quarters, she'd spend a few evenings a week with me. It's been too quiet without her."

No matter how hard I'd tried, I couldn't wrap my head around the warped relationship between Silas and Elsa. Talk about toxic and unhealthy. He'd slaughtered her parents and sister, forced her brother to be a killer, but she adored Silas? It just didn't compute. If you asked me, the girl needed some serious psychological help. Was she blind to what he truly was? I guessed possessing the morals of a scorpion on acid was undoubtedly a side effect of being raised by him.

"I'll tell her you're expecting her this evening."

He nodded as he sat behind his desk. "Now that A36 is here, our plans for expansion can proceed. The deadline was yesterday. How many other territories have accepted my proposal?"

I cleared my throat. "As of this morning, two more."

He raised an eyebrow. "Only two? What about the others?"

"Adria and Galena declined."

He leaned back into the soft leather of his chair and crossed his legs. Silas didn't handle rejection well, and I knew he wouldn't let this go. He'd wear down their leaders—or blackmail them—until they accepted. "I'll make an offer to their seconds in command later this week. Make preliminary plans for C24 to deal with the current heads of Galena and Adria."

"Of course." Since Asher was detained three months ago, Silas had wasted no time in implementing his expansion plans. He'd offered genetic harvesting to several surrounding territories. For a hefty price, of course. The heads of those areas were given a deadline to respond. Some of them had balked and cut off all contact with the Colony, whether over money or ethics. Others had jumped at the offer. Those who'd accepted also regularly engaged the services of our young operatives. The leaders who declined had no idea Silas's plan was to have them eliminated and succeeded by someone who bought into the Colony's way of life. Silas was determined to win one way or the other. "Will that be all?"

"Just one more thing." His basilisk eyes gleamed in excitement. Which made me want to gird my loins in dread of what could make him this happy. "A36 is waiting for you in your office. He's ready for an assignment."

"H-he's ready?" A cold ball of fear weighed heavy in my stomach. Not only fear for Asher, but also for the innocent people he'd be unleashed on. "But Asher was nowhere near—"

"Asher is gone. There is only A36 now."

His features hardened, and I detected the hint of challenge in his eyes. Did he question where I stood? Even a shred of doubt could send my plan up in flames. There'd be nothing left of me but a pile of ashes, and Silas standing over me with a wicked smile of victory.

"Of course. I'll get him prepped and out on assignment."

Silas smiled. "See that you do." He waved his hand as if shooing me away, indicating our meeting was over. As I closed my data pad, his gaze froze on my hands, and an expression of distaste twisted his features. "Declan, you really shouldn't bite your nails. Such a nasty habit. Take care of that immediately."

"Yes, sir," I replied, shoving my hands in my pockets. There were plenty of nasty habits in the Colony, but all things considered, mine was the least of the evils.

●　　●　　●

I left Silas's office for my own. What he'd said disturbed me, and a twinge of apprehension niggled at a corner of my mind. Asher was gone? What did that even mean? Surely Silas meant we no longer referred to Ash by his real name. My friend—I still considered him that even if I'd been permanently barred from his friend zone—had very much been himself a few days ago. Distraught and shattered, but still the gallant hero bent on saving the world.

Several people nodded in greeting as I passed. Being in Silas's upper echelon had changed the way people looked at me. Those who'd previously disregarded me now sought out my favor in an attempt to further their own standing. I'd never received so many social event invitations in my life. And every one of them sickened me. Sure, I attended the occasional dinner party, but it was only to keep up appearances. Being too much of a party boy would be frowned upon, but for political reasons, I couldn't refuse everyone. Everything I did was to maintain the illusion.

The attendees discussed purchasing more genes to change their appearance as if they were making a casual weekly visit to the market. They judged and remarked on the attributes of other citizens as if appearance were a contest. They complained about the lack of popular products—which meant donors weren't being murdered quickly enough for their tastes. Keeping a smile plastered on my face while pretending to agree with them was one of the greatest challenges I'd ever faced. They may have been physical perfection on the outside, but inside they were empty. Void of anything human. What kind of existence was that? To me, life was meant to be messy, imperfect, full of peaks and valleys. It was the ultimate journey, and I wouldn't have it any other way.

After passing more of the shallow vessels impersonating humans, I finally reached my office. I swung open the door and halted. Hairs rose on the back of my neck.

I was afraid to move a muscle.

To even breathe.

Casually leaning against my desk, ankles crossed, was a dangerous predator. He watched me intently. Muscles rippled in his forearms as he flipped a silver dagger in one hand.

It was Asher. But it wasn't.

Sure, Ash had killed before, but it was to save hostages or in self-defense. He'd never outright murder anyone with no justification. But I sensed the creature in front of me was on a wholly different level. To him, killing was the same as eating or sleeping. It was routine, a part of life, something he did every day. And didn't think twice about.

A36 stood before me.

He assessed me from head to toe, gauging my level of threat. I was riveted by the way the dagger glinted as it caught the sunlight streaming in through the window. Captivated by how A36 managed to catch the handle every time without even looking at it. If he determined me a danger, that blade could be thrust into my chest before I took my next breath.

He caught the dagger for the last time, sheathed it at his waist, then finally broke his gaze. I'd been weighed and discarded. A36 believed in survival of the fittest and between the two of us, there was no question about who would be left standing.

Silas hadn't been lying when he'd said Asher was gone. I didn't know what provoked the change in him, but the selfless team leader who risked his life rescuing hostages at harvest facilities had been replaced by a stone-cold, heartless killer.

"You're Declan." Even his voice was different. Flat. Emotionless. Just like his eyes.

I sidestepped him and kept as much distance between us as possible to get to my desk. My skin prickled being this close to him. "Yes. Why don't you sit down, A36?"

"No. I want my assignment."

"I have it, but we need to go over—"

"We need to go over nothing. Don't waste my time."

An all-action, no-talk kind of guy. A killing machine to be set in motion. I didn't want to be the one to unleash him, but I had no choice. When I was unable to get to him while he was in training these three months, I'd hoped by the time Silas released him I'd have a plan in place with the Insurgents. I didn't, and my time was up. All I could hope to do at this point was to minimize the casualties.

I opened my data pad and pulled up the file Silas had sent me. "I just forwarded it to you. You'll be accompanied by ten other soldiers."

"They're under my command?"

"Yes. But you're not to use deadly force unless absolutely necessary. Do you understand, A36?" He glared at me in stony silence, but I could tell by the tightening of his jaw he wanted to challenge that order. "Do you understand?" I asked more forcefully.

"Affirmative," he muttered. "Are we done?"

"Yes. Report back to me when your mission is completed."

A36 gave a curt nod, then strode out the door, closing it behind him. I exhaled loudly and slumped back in my chair. Getting Paige to meet with me was now more important than ever. Lives were literally at stake. The missions would keep coming, and A36 would continue to kill. No matter his orders, I had the feeling he considered them more like flexible guidelines. He'd stray outside the boundaries at his leisure. Maybe just to spice up his day. And there was no way to stop him. No one had the stones to stand in his way. Restraining him wasn't an option.

Once A36 was gone, Asher could never live with himself knowing what he'd done. The sooner I could get to Paige, the more people we could save, and the less blood Asher would have on his hands.

Also, I'm not sure what his thinking was, but he'd cut his hair. Shorn himself nearly bald. Brynn would have a fit when she saw it. He looked more intimidating, a quality that already seeped from every pore of A36's body, and it was surely less of a bother during missions. But seriously, what a waste of good hair.

6

BRYNN

I winced as I tugged the shirt over my head. My chest wound had healed, but the area around it was still tender. And it chafed me to no end. After three months, I still wasn't anywhere near one hundred percent physically despite training for hours every day. Mom said I needed to give my body time to heal, that I was pushing myself too hard. Screw that. I needed to be ready at a moment's notice, and I was determined my body wouldn't fail me when I needed it most.

Wouldn't fail him.

Asher was depending on me.

I trotted down the stairs, out the back door, then warmed up for my daily five-mile run. It helped clear my mind and sometimes inspired ideas to help the Insurgents. On fantastic days, I came up with exciting new ways to kill Silas. Today, my mind dredged up painful memories from three months ago.

When Mom had suddenly appeared at my bedside the night we'd escaped, I'd thought it was the pain meds, hallucinations, or a dream. But it was none of those. My mother had been miraculously returned to me. During an operation horribly gone wrong, we'd believed she died in the field alongside my father after they'd sacrificed themselves to save the rest of our team. Because she was a gifted physician, the Colony wanted her skills, so she'd been held against her will and forced to work for them ever since. She'd never tried to contact us for fear we'd try to rescue her and endanger our own lives. And she was right. We'd have moved mountains to get her back.

After a brief, tearful reunion, she'd told me that night we were finally getting the hell out of the Colony.

"You told him? Ash knows I'm alive?" I gingerly swung my legs over the side of the bed.

"Yes, baby, he knows." Mom slid pants over my legs and pulled them up as I slowly stood upright. I hated feeling like an invalid. "But I'm not so sure he believed me. Seeing you will be the only way to prove it. Ash is stubborn, but he loves you something fierce."

I grinned as she slipped a sweatshirt over my head. "Yeah. He does." Remembering the last time I'd seen him, the look on Asher's face when he thought I was dying—when *I'd* believed I was dying—ripped through me with the force of an avalanche. And for days he'd known no different, thinking the Colony had killed me and he was left alone to face a life without me.

I'd begged anyone who'd listen to let me see him or get word to him I'd survived. No one even spoke to me. Meds were administered, food was delivered, and assistance was given with showering and dressing, but that was the extent of my contact with others. I was out of my mind with worry for him and what he'd do to anyone who got too close.

Or to himself.

Mom told me Ash had killed Everly. I hoped it was a lengthy, agonizing death and wished I'd been there to help or at least watch and cheer him on. But he'd snapped her neck, quick and painless. After that, he'd fought his way to my room with the slim hope we could escape. The odds were heaped against us, but Asher wasn't ready to give up. That day I witnessed him slay every soldier who dared to come through my door.

Correction. A36 slayed them.

Mom slipped the jacket over my shoulders and zipped it up. "Let's go, Brynn. Your brother and Ash are waiting for us." Her voice was hurried but confident, laced with undertones of excitement. She was leaving this godforsaken city of narcissism after years of imprisonment, and finally being reunited with her family. Minus Dad.

With her arm around me for support, we moved swiftly down the darkened corridors lit only by emergency lighting. I'd be eternally grateful for whoever cut the power for us. Possibly even give them my firstborn. If there ever was one.

Rounding the corner to the last hallway, Mom said, "We're in the final stretch, Brynn. They're waiting for us just beyond that door."

Mom seemed unconcerned, but my internal danger monitor pinged like crazy. We'd encountered no one since leaving my room. Not a single guard or civilian. It seemed too easy, and that didn't sit right with me. Every instinct shouted something was wrong, but I pushed my suspicions aside because my need to get out of that place eclipsed everything else. We were so close. Knowing I'd see Ash and Noah in seconds filled my body with the strength I needed to go just a little further.

Mom shoved the door open. Freedom. I tilted my face up to the darkening sky and gulped fresh air for the first time in months.

"Evening, Anna. Nice night for an escape, don't you think?"

We froze. Colonel Ackerman stood in front of us, chin held high, eyes gleaming in triumph. Behind him, two soldiers held between them a silently seething Noah, neck veins bulging, wrists bound.

My heart stopped.

The Colony knew Mom, Asher, and I were leaving. They knew Noah was meeting us. They knew everything.

Ackerman's broad shoulders were nearly twice the width of Noah's leaner frame. He'd been Everly's right hand. Hatred and disgust welled up inside me at what the two of them had done to Ash and me. Asher had already killed Everly. It seemed to reason Ackerman's fate was left to me. His future didn't look bright.

Just over a week post-surgery from my chest wound, I wasn't good for much, but I was down for a fight. The Colony had taken away too much of my life already, and I'd resolved to die before letting them lock me up again.

Mom tried to push me behind her, but I wasn't having it. "Colonel Ackerman, please. Just let my children go, and you can have me. I'll go peacefully with you."

"No!" Noah lunged toward us. The female soldier shoved a gun into his ribs and jerked his shoulder back.

Ackerman grinned, clearly enjoying himself. "No need to offer yourself in exchange for them. You're all free to go, compliments of Director Reeves."

Mom narrowed her eyes and cocked her head. "Free to go? We can walk out the gates and you'll do nothing to stop us." She didn't believe him any more than I did. It was like putting our faith in a tiger who hadn't eaten for days and trusting him not to devour us.

I looked at Noah. He shook his head slightly, letting me know he felt the same. If we attempted to leave, one or all of us would get a bullet to the back of the head. It couldn't be that simple. There had to be a catch.

And then I knew.

"Where's Asher?" I demanded.

Ackerman trained his triumphant gaze on me and feigned surprise. "You mean Subject A36? He won't be making the journey with you. He opted to stay and work for us."

"You lying piece of—" A stab of pain in my chest cut off my words and stole my breath.

Mom shook her head. "No. There's no way Asher would voluntarily stay here. I spoke to him myself."

Ackerman shrugged. "People change their minds." His expression hardened. "A36 stays here."

"You mean he's staying so we can go free."

"Believe what you want, Anna. A36 belongs to the Colony. He goes where Director Reeves sends him." Ackerman turned to my brother, cut his restraints, then shoved him in our direction. Noah rubbed his wrists as he staggered over, then drew both of us into a quick hug.

"A touching reunion. But I'd advise not wasting any time. The director's generous offer isn't open-ended. We can always escort the three of you back inside."

My stomach roiled in protest at the thought of leaving Asher here. I knew in the depths of my soul he'd never stay unless he had no choice. He'd traded his life for ours. For our freedom.

But not if I could help it. "We're not leaving here without Asher," I growled.

"Then you're not leaving." Ackerman's eyes narrowed. His expression turned stony, daring me to make a move.

Mom spun around to face me. Her voice was urgent, but low so only Noah and I could hear. "Brynn, we have to go. I promise we'll get Asher back, or he'll fight his way out of here and find us, but we have to go while we have the chance."

I clenched my hands into fists and spoke through gritted teeth. "Ash would never leave me here, and I *will not* abandon him." Yes, he'd want me to go, to be free of the gates of the Colony. He would shove me through them himself if he were here. But if the tables were turned, I knew without a doubt he'd never leave me behind.

Mom's eyes darted to my right in Noah's direction, and a silent communication passed between them.

He slid one arm around my back while his other swept behind my legs, then he scooped me up. I kicked and punched at his face, but still weak from surgery, my blows had the strength of a child. Rage filled my bloodstream at my inability to fight back. My body had never failed me. I'd never felt so helpless. I wanted to rip Ackerman apart, make him hurt in every cell of his body and scream for mercy.

I cursed Noah for taking away my control.

"No!" I screamed, still struggling against my brother.

Ackerman snickered in amusement. "You've got your hands full with her, Anna. She's a feisty one. Might want to keep an eye on her."

"*You* might want to count your blessings she's not at her best right now, Ackerman. You wouldn't be standing if she were."

He let out a snort. "I admit she's a challenge, but nowhere near my level."

"Not at the moment, anyway." Mom gave him a knowing smile, full of confidence. "Don't make that same assumption about Asher. He'll destroy you if he thinks you harmed a hair on her head. And you know he can do it. I suspect you're already on his radar after what you and Everly did."

The cocky smile on Ackerman's face slid away at her words. The glint of fear in his eyes was a minor salve on my wounded pride, but I'd take what I could get.

Mom had spent years behind these gates separated from her family. I'd spent months here against my will, used to manipulate Asher to carry out Everly's wishes. With Noah carrying me and Mom watching our backs, we strode through the gates of the Colony, free at last.

Angry tears streamed down my face, and I felt something shatter deep inside as I left part of me, maybe the best part, behind.

That was three months ago. Mom, Noah, and I had been in hiding ever since. Glancing at the watch on my arm, I noted my pace was better than on yesterday's run. I increased my speed even more.

After our release, we'd been afraid Silas would track us and didn't want to lead him to the new Insurgent location. Instead, we'd traveled to an old safe house to plan our next move. And how we'd get Asher back.

The Colony wanted A36, but that's not who he truly was. Sure, he could kill. As A36, he'd taken the lives of those soldiers who'd entered my room in a cold, detached manner. They'd meant as much to him as the color of paint on the walls. But Asher had still been in control. Once he knew we were safe, rather than become that person again and let A36 take over completely, I knew he'd try to take his own life.

But he was a valuable weapon, one that had cost millions. With numerous failed trials, Asher had taken over a decade to develop, and over another decade to locate after his father, Garrett, had stolen him away from the lab where Asher had been created. Mom, Noah, and I were his Achilles heel, so I was convinced Silas was still threatening us in some capacity to ensure he followed orders. I just hadn't figured out how. There's no way Silas could know our location. We'd been vigilant and careful when we fled the Colony. No one had followed us.

Once settled, we'd contacted Paige. She was acting Controller in Noah's absence. With our compound destroyed, it had taken time to locate and set up a new base of operations for our sector. Xander, who'd previously worked in our sector and now ran the safe house where we'd discovered Asher's true identity, had put out feelers and come up with a place. It was an old, abandoned schoolhouse about ten miles from our destroyed compound. Plenty of rooms, a designated cafeteria, and a gym for training. Perfect.

Too many of our operatives had been killed during the attack. Paige shouldered a heavy load right now with rebuilding, recruiting, training, and carrying out missions with the skeleton crew remaining. Other sectors had sent as many operatives and support staff as they could spare, but things had been tough for her. My brother Noah, while drowning in self-pity, had done absolutely nothing to help, even after Xander moved us to another house within a reasonable distance from Paige's new location so we could connect with their sector.

After years of working for the Colony, Mom was still reaching out to the contacts she'd established within their organization and in the city itself. I'd been shocked to hear some of those self-absorbed parasites actually had a soul, but she said there was an underground working against

Silas. They'd wanted to join efforts with the Insurgents for quite a while but had no idea how to go about it and stay under the radar. And stay alive in the process. She had to move slowly so as not to draw attention to us or our location, but her goal was to unite those groups. We'd take all the help we could get, and anyone inside the gates would be an added benefit.

Noah was on my last nerve. He'd been about as useful as the fungus on the fallen tree I jumped over. I checked my watch again. My pace had picked up.

His failure to confirm Declan's identity and background of working in Barton's sector had contributed to the destruction of our compound, the loss of many lives, and my kidnapping. Yeah, he'd not only dropped the ball, he'd also deflated and destroyed it. But we all made mistakes, and there was no way he could have foreseen the repercussions of that indiscretion. After he, Mom, and I left the Colony that night, he'd become a different person. Someone I didn't recognize. He'd spent the last three months reading, lying around the safe house, and had basically turned into a misery-spewing fountain. Black clouds hovered around him.

Mom and I had reiterated over and over that even if he'd discovered Declan was really Oz, the Colony already had the information about our location and the attack would have happened no matter what. The deal was done. Our reassurances made no difference to him. In his mind, he'd failed. Failed me and the operatives who'd died defending the compound. Failed our father's expectations and legacy.

Most of all he'd failed himself and Asher. His best friend. His brother.

His warped self-perception had rendered him all but paralyzed when it came to making decisions. He'd lost all faith in himself and his ability to make sound judgements or strategize.

It was maddening to see my once confident brother, mature beyond his years and previously in a position of leadership over people nearly twice his age, reduced to someone whose biggest daily decision was which shirt to wear or what book to read. Mom, Paige, and I tried but couldn't persuade him to forgive himself, get off his ass, and go back to work. He was wasting his talents, and I had to wonder how much more progress we'd have made by now if he'd joined in our efforts.

When I finished my run, I entered the back door of our house, grabbed a towel from the kitchen counter, then wiped sweat from my face. After refilling my water bottle, I went in search of my brother and hoped against all odds that he'd done something productive today.

Instead, he was sprawled on the couch, reading a book.

In the flip of a switch, my feel-good exercise endorphins mutated into flaming balls of rage. I stomped over to him, then ripped the novel from his hands. "Seriously, Noah? This is how you're spending your time? Asher stayed at the Colony to keep us safe, gave up everyone he loved, and you pay him back by reading some book of the month?" I tossed it into the empty fireplace. I wished it had been filled with a roaring fire that burned the book to ashes.

He didn't even try to stop me from taking it or retrieve it from the fireplace. Rising to a sitting position, he ran his hands over his closely shorn hair, then looked up at me. His expression was empty. Lost. What happened to the Noah who was always strategizing? Calculating his opponents' moves and keeping at least one step ahead of them? I barely recognized my sloth-like brother whose only interests besides books seemed to be taking long walks to who-knew-where or staring into space at an empty wall.

Letting out a heavy breath, he finally spoke. "I know exactly what he gave up. I think about it every day, Brynn. Every minute. I think about how I'm the reason we're in this position. How so many Insurgents, people who trusted me to lead them, are dead because of my mistake. Your kidnapping and near death? My fault. Trust me, I know better than anyone what Ash sacrificed for us. If I'd made one simple call to Barton, taken five minutes out of my day, none of us would be in this situation."

"You screwed up, Noah." I threw my hands in the air. "You're human. But I'm so freaking tired of repeating this conversation with you every few days. Whether you discovered Declan's identity or not, the Colony was going to attack us. It happened. Move on and do something about it."

His face was incredulous, like I was speaking nonsense or a language he didn't understand. "*I'm* sick of telling *you*. You still don't get it. I can't be trusted to make judgement calls for myself or for anyone else. I'm no help to anyone at this point."

I rolled my eyes. "Quit being such a drama queen and get over yourself. Yeah, you made a bad decision. One that affected a lot of people, but that's one crappy decision out of hundreds of good ones that saved a lot of lives and prevented our operatives from being injured or killed. Stop letting a single mistake define you. People make errors in judgement every day, but life still goes on."

Noah closed his eyes and shook his head. "I'd only get more people hurt, and I can't handle anymore failure."

Frustration coursed through me. He was wasting time, and I didn't have the patience to listen to anymore of his whining. "If Asher and I weren't captured by the Colony, we might never have found out Mom was still alive. Because of her, we've connected with the underground in the Colony, people who are with us in the fight. Something good still came out of all the destruction. But now? Asher would be so disappointed if he saw what's happened to you." This would hit below the belt and be incredibly painful, but maybe it would jar him out of this funk he'd been wallowing in for weeks. I took a deep breath before I said it. "And so would Dad."

His face crumpled. "You think I don't know that?" Noah bolted from the sofa over to the fireplace, then turned to face me. "I know what people think of me, and I can feel Dad's disappointment in me from his grave!" His voice was full of anger instead of the infuriating apathetic tone that made me want to punch him. Now we were getting somewhere.

I stalked over to him and stood toe to toe, looked up and met his anguished gaze. "Good. At least you're finally feeling something. Getting back to work will help heal those wounds, Noah. We need you. Asher needs you. If you were missing, don't you think he'd move Heaven and Earth to find you?"

His mouth tightened. Something flashed behind his eyes like the beginning of a storm. "He would."

"You owe him the same courtesy. Do something, Noah." I flung my arms out to the side. "Anything but this."

He glared at me a long moment, then shouldered past me. The back door slammed behind him.

At least it was a start.

7

PAIGE

I couldn't believe he'd contacted me. Not after everything he'd done. So much death and destruction because of the way Declan felt about me. So many lives altered and ended over something so trivial. Trivial to me, anyway. I'd never be able to return his feelings. First of all, he had the wrong equipment, something he was unaware of, but more importantly he'd put himself before so many others and become one of the mindless barbarians inside the Colony.

I used to be one of those people. Certainly not by choice. My life had been one of ignorance, clueless about the actions of the community where I lived. When I'd learned my parents had me genetically altered at a very young age, understood the atrocities committed in the name of vanity, I'd been furious. We'd all exchanged hurtful words. There was not a shred of regret on my part, and I honestly didn't care about how my parents felt. I'd cut them off, packed up that same night while they slept, then walked out. I hadn't seen them since and didn't care to. The daughter born to them wasn't good enough. My appearance was unacceptable, imperfect, and I'd been stripped of choices that would affect my life forever. Knowing people were sacrificed just to give me more appealing physical traits repulsed me.

Joining the Insurgents was the best decision I'd ever made. Agreeing to meet with Declan could be the worst. Months later, we still dealt with the fallout of his ruinous, utterly selfish decision. Asher robbed of his freedom and forced to commit acts worse than anything conjured in my nightmares. Brynn still healing from a nearly fatal injury. We'd lost our compound and were just getting settled into our new location. Our operative numbers had been nearly cut in half, and most of the new recruits weren't ready for the field. The operatives sent from other sectors had been a godsend, but we still weren't operating at the level we had before Declan. In my mind, I referred to anything that occurred before that day as BD—Before Declan. It allowed me to avoid saying his name any more than I had to.

And Noah. He'd always been a strong, competent, decisive leader, and I'd respected him immensely as my Controller. I hadn't seen that man in months. What was left was someone who looked and sounded like him, but all the traits that made him a strong leader had been destroyed along with the compound. I'd assumed the role of interim Controller when Noah had traveled to the Colony with Asher after Brynn was kidnapped. At his request, I'd stayed in that role when he'd returned with his sister and mother. Even if he hadn't asked, I wouldn't have relinquished the helm. Not to the empty shell he was now. According to Brynn, Noah had the decision-making skills of a drunken weasel. Whatever that meant. I hoped my friend and leader would make peace with himself and return soon. We desperately needed him.

Declan had contacted Elijah on some private channel the two of them had set up when he'd still been Oz. My first instinct was to say we'd meet when hell froze over, and if he came anywhere near us, he could count on getting to said location sooner rather than later. With what he'd done, I was certain it was his final destination. Then the more logical voice in my head stopped me. Declan was in the Colony. With Ash's fate uncertain, I couldn't afford to make any rash decisions.

Which was why I'd requested a meeting with Anna, Brynn, and Noah to get their input. They were my most trusted consultants.

Dry autumn leaves and twigs crunched beneath my feet as I trekked to our meeting place. As a precaution, we never met at our new compound or at their safehouse. On the off chance we were being watched, we didn't want to lead any unwanted visitors to either location. An early morning mist swirled around my ankles, and birds twittered from the trees overhead. Such a beautiful day tempted me to take a break and enjoy it, but with all the ongoing atrocities, I didn't have time to rest. Since the day

I'd escaped the Colony, I'd done everything I could to put an end to their acts, and I wouldn't stop until their reign ended.

Arriving at the clearing first, I scouted the area for any interlopers. Extra care had saved me more than once. Once I'd secured it, I sat on a moss-covered rock that jutted out from a craggy formation while I waited. Closing my eyes, I listened to the sounds around me, searching for anything out of the ordinary. Moments later, birds scattered overhead, and I detected the subtle rustling of bushes from my left. I opened my eyes to see Brynn entering the clearing, Anna close behind her, and Noah bringing up the rear. Brynn's gaze darted around the area, the hand not poised on the gun in her holster clenching and unclenching. Always on guard, that one. I missed being in the field with her, that certainty of knowing she had my back no matter what happened.

Noah's shoulders curved inward, his fists shoved deep in the pockets of the calf-length dark tan leather coat I'd always admired. He looked as if he'd rather be anywhere else.

A wide smile slid across Anna's face as she approached me, and she opened her arms. I'd never been a fan of physical contact, but I could never turn down Anna's hugs. After believing her to be dead these past years, I'd vowed to never take them for granted again. Rising from the rock, I eagerly returned her embrace. "Hello, sweetheart," she whispered.

Her miraculous reappearance was the silver lining in a Pandora's box full of disaster and sadness. She held me tightly, and I allowed myself to relax just for this moment. I fleetingly wondered what my life might have been like if my own parents had been anything like Anna and Patrick. They accepted their children as they were and loved them fiercely, flaws and all. Mine had replaced any of my physical attributes they considered flaws. Anna filled the deep void I hadn't known was there, and I was so grateful to have her back in my life. Since she'd interacted with Declan before leaving the Colony, I needed her help in setting aside my personal feelings about him and remaining objective before making this decision.

Brynn nodded at me, swung a leg over a fallen tree, and then straddled it as her seat. Noah remained standing, his gaze fixed on the ground.

Anna released me and stepped back. "So, what's going on, Paige? Please tell me it's not bad news."

"I don't see how it could be good. It's about Declan."

Brynn's eyes narrowed, and her jaw hardened. Noah's head snapped up, his face frozen in anguish. "He's sent word he wants to meet with me."

"No. Absolutely not. Whatever that filthy piece of—"

"Brynn." Anna interrupted.

Considering the word Anna had cut off, it seemed clear Brynn's and my thoughts on Declan were aligned. After everything he'd done, I wanted to believe the bridges were burned and irreparable, but I reminded myself again he was inside the Colony and had eyes on Asher. We needed every advantage we could get. Even if it came from a lowlife like Declan.

Anna's gaze rested a moment on each of us before she spoke. "What Declan did was horrific, that goes without saying. The Oz I knew would never have considered giving such sensitive information to our enemies. However, when we were at the Colony and he told me who he'd been and what he'd done, Declan was full of remorse. He was overcome with guilt and grief and had no idea of the magnitude of his actions and what they would lead to. His only objective was to set things right and he begged me to let him help us escape."

"Full of remorse?" Brynn snapped. "I'd bet he's the reason Silas knew about our escape. There's *nothing* he could do to make up for the damage he's caused. He cost us nearly everything. He cost us Asher." Her voice caught on Asher's name, and the air around her sparked with hatred for Declan.

Anna leveled her gaze on Brynn. "Asher had the chance to kill him when Everly threw them in the sparring ring together. She wanted him to end Declan's life, tried to goad him into it. No doubt A36 wanted to fulfill her wish, but Ash spared him. Don't you trust his instincts?"

Her words had the desired effect, and doubt flashed across Brynn's face so quickly I wondered if I'd imagined it. Anna's words also gave me pause. Asher's instincts were usually right on target. A36 had made his first appearance during the attack on our compound when Brynn was kidnapped. I'd witnessed his violent slaughter of Colony soldiers and his vow to end Declan's life the next time they met. Even now as I remembered the cold rage in Ash's voice chills skittered down my spine. I'd honestly believed that was the last time I'd ever see Declan alive. But when given the chance to fulfill that promise, Ash hadn't killed him. I had to trust he had a good reason.

"Noah?" Anna asked. His eyebrows lifted in surprise. "What are your thoughts?"

He leaned against a tree, arms crossed. Rays of early morning sunlight broke through the canopy of leaves and cast a bronze glow over his dark brown skin. "I can't make a judgement call on this. Look where it got us last time."

"Not this again," Brynn mumbled.

"He fooled us all, Noah," I said in what I hoped was a reassuring tone. "Declan gave us no reason to suspect him of anything. You can't place all the blame on your shoulders."

He huffed out a breath. "Brynn knew something was off about him."

I rolled my eyes. "She thinks there's something off about nearly everyone."

Brynn furrowed her brow, considered my words, then shrugged. "You're not wrong."

"Noah." Anna's tone was soft but firm. Her absence hadn't allowed her to witness Noah as Controller and the effortless way he'd slipped into the position after Patrick died, but she knew her son. No matter the previous events, she still trusted his judgement. And clearly expected an answer.

His gaze flicked to the ground, and his arms tightened over his chest, like he was hugging himself for reassurance. It was clear he warred with his internal thoughts for a long period, but finally answered his mother. "You said he helped you and Brynn. That he was supposed to go to Asher's room and transport him to the morgue."

Anna nodded.

"But we can't be sure he followed through with that plan. Asher never came out."

"I know he got Asher on the stretcher and was on the way to the morgue. He messaged me to let me know."

"He could have been lying. Maybe he went back on his word and turned Asher in. We can't be certain."

"If he'd tried to prevent Ash from leaving that night, Declan wouldn't be alive," Brynn said. "The three of us were used for leverage to keep Ash there. That's the only reason he stayed."

Noah looked at me in question. "If the Colony knew Declan helped us, then why is he still alive? Are you certain it was him that contacted you?"

Anna replied for me. "My contact says Silas is unaware of Declan's involvement and depends heavily on him. Declan is part of his inner circle. Another man was blamed for assisting us and paid the price. I believe that was Declan's doing."

I shook my head. "If he's working so closely with Silas, this has to be a trap. He wants to learn the location of our new compound or wants to take one or all of you back to the Colony."

Anna furrowed her brow. "I can't speak about the Declan from before. All I have to go on is the boy who came to me so wrought with guilt he was nearly broken. He helped us that night. Asher trusted him for a reason, and our options are limited. I don't think we should be too hasty to turn down help where we can get it, Paige. You may not want to hear this," she said, side-eyeing Brynn, "but I think he might want to work for us on the inside. If that's the case, he could know more about Asher than any of my informants."

Brynn shot to her feet. "Declan as our inside guy? He probably figures they're on to him, and he's hoping to cut his losses and worm his way back into our good graces. Not happening."

"That's my first reaction, too," I nodded, hoping the calm in my voice would tamp down her anger. "I struggled with this, Brynn. When Elijah told me Declan had reached out, I wanted to shut him down immediately. I debated even bringing this to the three of you. The thought of seeing him again, let alone working with him, repulses me. But on the outside chance he has something to offer and genuinely wants to help us? Well, he's in a prime position to do it. I don't think we can afford to turn him down."

Anna leaned against the rock I perched on. I enjoyed having her close. She radiated comfort and calm that flowed into those around her. Well, maybe not into Brynn at the moment, but comfort and calm were two things I could certainly use more of. Like a fire warming my chilled body on a wintery day. Being Controller wasn't a simple job. I was happy to do it for now, but when Noah was ready, I'd gladly hand the reins back to him. I missed the action in the field and interacting with the kids we rescued. My current duties didn't allow me to spend time with them during their brief stay at our compound.

But I was Controller. This was a huge decision, one not to be taken lightly. If the other Insurgents got wind we were working with Declan, I could have a mutiny on my hands. They weren't in the frame of mind to forgive and forget. Frankly, neither was I. The wounds he'd inflicted were still jagged and bleeding. On the other hand, if his efforts were sincere, Anna was correct in saying we shouldn't turn him away. Especially if the source was that close to Silas.

Noah raised his downcast eyes and spoke first. "I think we should trust him. Not because my gut is saying so, but because Mom has faith in him."

Brynn stared at Anna a couple beats. She had more personal stake in this than any of us. "I'm willing to give him a chance. But not because of what your contact said or what Declan told you. I based my decision solely on the fact that Asher didn't kill him when he had a chance. My faith is in him. Always."

I nodded. "So is mine. I'll reach out to Declan and let you know when the meeting is scheduled."

Brynn got a wicked gleam in her eye. "I'd like to be there."

"I don't think that's such a good idea," Anna replied.

"Try and stop me." She smirked.

Anna sighed heavily. "Fine. At least give the boy a chance to speak, Brynn."

Upon waking this morning, I'd had no intention of seriously considering meeting with the man who'd behaved so selfishly and given no regard to the consequences of his actions. Less than an hour with Anna, Brynn, and Noah had changed my entire perspective. I'd have sooner believed the trees surrounding us could turn into giants and amble away.

DECLAN

I leaned against the bumper of my Jeep and scanned the surrounding forest. Right now, all was quiet except for the occasional chattering of squirrels and birds chirping overhead. Paige had agreed to meet in an area close to one of the Colony's harvest facilities. I had no idea where my former sector had relocated and didn't want to know. Not yet anyway. That's why we were meeting off a back road in the middle of nowhere.

The donor numbers at this particular harvest facility had been low recently, and I told Silas I'd make a trip to check into the problem. It was just a cover story so I could meet Paige. The source of the problem wasn't a mystery.

It was me.

I'd been feeding the Insurgents transport schedules, and they'd been rescuing hostages en route to this facility. I'd remained anonymous, but after several tipoffs, they knew my information was reliable. There was no way Silas could trace the information back to me. I was grateful every day for the sneaky tech skills Elijah had taught me that allowed me to cover my tracks. I'd hacked into areas I had no clearance for, retrieved what I needed, then backed out, leaving no trace of my visit. Kind of like a cyber ninja. I smirked.

After stretching my arms overhead, I checked the time again. Despite her reassurance, I wasn't convinced Paige would show. Not until I saw her with my own eyes. Sure, she'd sent confirmation of our meeting—but still. There was bad blood and history between us. If she came, I'd be eternally grateful she was willing to hear me out. Forgiveness wasn't bundled with her decision to meet. I knew that. The whole thing could blow up in my face. Snipers stationed in the trees could have me in their sights right now.

At that thought, I hunched my shoulders and peered into the overhead branches.

If she was able set aside her personal feelings for me, she'd see how valuable I could be to the Insurgents. Paige was a strategic thinker and certainly wasn't lacking in intelligence. I just needed to convince her to give me a chance.

"Hands up."

My spine stiffened. The voice came from behind me, off to the right. I knew that voice. Its owner had barked orders at me, ridiculed me, and given me nightmares—but had also saved my life more than once. No doubt she had a clear shot to the back of my head.

Brynn.

Had Paige come with her?

Brynn moved like a stealthy lion on the prowl. I hadn't even heard her approach. She didn't have an itchy trigger finger, but I didn't want to do anything to set her off. I rose slowly, arms raised, and turned in her direction. Paige stood beside her. The sight of her took my breath away. Underneath it all, I still thought of her as a friend. Her cold, hardened expression told me she didn't return those feelings. No surprise there.

"You don't need the gun, Brynn. I'm not here to hurt anyone."

She barked out a laugh. "Fool me once, Declan. I halfway trusted you before and look where it got us. It's a mistake I won't repeat. Any sudden movements on your part, my pent-up aggression gets free rein."

While Brynn covered me, Paige approached me and then searched my body for weapons. And not in a gentle way. Admittedly, I'd been known to infringe upon the boundaries of stupidity, but I wasn't brainless enough to come to this meeting armed. I knew where that mistake would lead. My body lying in a pool of blood and someone—in this case, Brynn—standing over me with a satisfied grin on her face. Trust was my goal here, and packing heat wasn't the pathway to earn it.

"He's clean," Paige called over her shoulder to Brynn.

"Can I lower my hands now?"

Brynn shrugged. "Sure. But don't expect me to lower my gun."

"Understood." I dropped my hands slowly but kept them in full view. One suspicious move on my part and she'd shoot first and never ask any questions.

Paige stepped away from me and moved to stand beside Brynn. Her emerald eyes flashed a warning. "Anna vouching for you is the only reason I'm here. I trust her judgement. Don't you dare prove her wrong."

I nodded. "I'm here to help the Insurgents."

Brynn let out an exasperated sigh. "Stop wasting our time and get to the real reason you wanted this meeting."

I held my hands out in a pleading gesture. "I've given you no reason to believe me, I get that." Paige flashed an incredulous look at Brynn over that remark. "I'll spend the rest of my life trying to make up for what I did, but I know it will never be enough. Helping you and Anna escape was only the beginning."

"I consider that payment for everything my mom did for you over the years."

"I owe Anna a lot. But there's more you don't know about. Since you and Anna left, I've made myself indispensable to Silas. He has me visiting harvest sites and gives me high priority assignments."

Paige narrowed her eyes. "We heard. Why doesn't Silas know about your involvement with the escape?"

I grinned. "Elijah taught me some valuable tricks. I altered the security footage and made it look like someone else helped them, then I upped my cred by turning him in. Believe me, this guy didn't exactly have a clean rap sheet."

Brynn's voice was flat. "Neither is yours."

Her words stung but were well-deserved. I dropped my gaze and cleared my throat before speaking again. "Anyway, that, along with the information I gave Everly was enough to propel me up the ladder pretty quickly."

"Unbelievable." Paige shook her head. "You're using the deaths of Insurgents and the loss of our compound for more personal gain? Isn't it enough you traded all of us for your own vanity?"

I held my hands up in a placating gesture. "No, wait. This is coming out all wrong." Pull it together, I told myself. It's a miracle Paige and Brynn even came, and now you're blowing this chance. Don't screw it up. I took a deep breath and tried again. "Please. Just listen. I've been giving several of the sectors information about travel routes so they can hit the vans before the hostages even reach the harvest centers. I can't give away all of them, but enough to stay under the radar and avoid suspicion." I looked at Brynn, knowing this would hit her hard. "The biggest part of my duties is doling out assignments and following up with Subjects A36 and C24."

Paige's mouth fell open in surprise. Brynn dropped her gun to her side, and I saw a twinge of hope in her eyes. "You've seen Asher?"

I dreaded telling her the truth. How should I put this? I'd seen a cold, callous man whose every move was threatening. People cowered in corners as he passed if they couldn't backtrack in the opposite direction first. I'd read report after report of how he single-handedly and systematically eliminated targets in minutes. He was a machine who did nothing but eat, sleep, and kill.

How could I say any of this to Brynn? The man I knew bore no resemblance to the Asher she loved.

My voice softened. "No. I haven't seen Asher in months, Brynn. Now, there's only A36, and he's everything they engineered him to be. I'm really sorry."

Her eyes glistened, and she glanced away.

"I think Asher is still in there somewhere, but in order to survive and keep you, Anna, and Noah safe, he's allowed A36 to do what needed to be done."

Brynn shook her head. "But we're fine. Silas let us go so Ash would stay, and we've had no trouble from the Colony. Can't you tell him that? Let him know he can come home?"

"That's just it, Brynn. He has to stay for you to continue to be safe. You're being tracked."

She stared at me a long moment. When she spoke, her voice was wrapped in icy rage. "How? Are you saying Silas knows where we are right now? He's known since that night?"

I nodded. "You and Anna have trackers embedded under your skin. Noah is clean. He was never a prisoner."

Brynn lunged toward me, grabbed my collar, and held the gun under my chin. "Why are you just now telling me this? If you've really been working against Silas all this time, this is information we needed months ago."

I didn't fight her or try to resist in any way. My life depended on me remaining calm and gaining their trust. "I didn't know then. Silas just told me recently, and you wouldn't have believed me anyway. But I know how to deactivate it."

This was the pivotal moment. The sole reason I was here. I hadn't known Brynn would come with Paige, but her presence would speed up the timeline and save Paige from being the middleman. Now I could show Brynn the tracker myself. She could decide to trust me or send me packing. Or kill me, which she'd probably considered and planned fifty times in the past ten minutes.

Her eyes bored into mine, and I didn't dare break that connection. "Where is the tracker?" she hissed.

"At the base of your neck. The scar is small. You'd never notice it unless you knew what to look for." I swallowed hard. If my confession didn't win her over, I had nothing left. This was my Hail Mary.

Still holding the gun under my chin, she gestured to Paige. "Check it." She pushed Brynn's long, dark braids away from her neck, then looked at me in question.

A trickle of sweat slid down my back. "It's hidden under a small circle that will look like a freckle or a mole. It's flat, but close to the surface, so it's easy to remove."

"Paige?" Brynn asked.

"It's here."

"Are you sure?"

"It's the only mark on your neck. What do you want me to do?"

"Cut it out."

Paige pulled a knife from the sheath at her hip. She placed one hand on Brynn's shoulder, then pointed the knife at the base of her neck. "Hold still." Brynn grimaced as she gently sliced away the covering over the tracker. Using the end of her sleeve, Paige wiped at the base of Brynn's neck, then held the knife out. The tracker lay on one side of the blade. "He's not lying. Here it is."

Brynn narrowed her eyes, then released my shirt collar and dropped the gun back to her side as she turned to look at the tiny black dot. It was half the size of the head of an eraser. I let out a sigh of relief.

"You're sure this is the only one?" she demanded.

"Positive. I've seen the monitors myself and the tech confirmed there's only one on each of you. Anna's will be in the same spot. She's had hers for years without her knowledge, but it wasn't activated until that night you all left. You need to crush it to destroy it."

Paige walked over to a large rock lying at the base of a tree, placed the tracker on top of it, then stabbed it with the knife repeatedly until she shattered it. She and Brynn shared a look, some silent communication between them. I really hoped it was the decision to trust me and not disembowel me then leave me for dead. Wouldn't be the first time Brynn had threatened to do it.

"What do you want from us, Declan?" Paige asked. "What's your end game here?"

I licked my lips nervously. "I want to help you take down the Colony. I'm in the perfect position to do it. Use me."

Brynn stared at me evenly. "You said you have contact with Ash." I nodded. "With the trackers gone, Mom, Noah, and I will move to the new compound. Silas can no longer use us as leverage to keep Ash at the Colony. I want you to get that information to him."

I'd known if they made the decision to trust me, Brynn would request this once the trackers were destroyed. I wanted to grant her request and get Asher the hell out of there. But if I told A36 his family was safe, he'd joyfully cut me open and dissect all my internal organs. His only loyalty was to the Colony.

"I want to, Brynn, I swear, but it's not that easy. He's not Asher anymore. The only direction he takes from me is mission orders, and he knows those come from Silas. If I mentioned anything to him about his family, he might wait long enough to tell Silas before he killed me. But I doubt it."

Brynn rarely showed emotion—unless she was with Asher. The two of them weren't shy about any PDA. I'd always been envious of their relationship—well, not the way it was now—and hoped maybe someday the relationship gods would see fit to bestow their gifts on me. Outwardly, Brynn remained still, but I saw the way her eyes tightened and the unmistakable anguish at knowing what Asher's life had become.

"You mentioned C24," Paige said. "Who is that? Wasn't Asher the only survivor of Project Adam?"

Wow. I'd forgotten they didn't know about Elsa. Her name may not mean anything to Paige, but Brynn had known her and spent nearly every day with Asher since his sisters' disappearance. This would come as a shock. "He was," I said slowly. "C24 is someone Silas has trained from a young age. He treats her like a daughter. She'd be as lethal as A36 if she had all his enhancements."

Paige bristled at my words.

"She's Asher's sister."

Brynn staggered backward and grabbed onto the hood of my Jeep to steady herself.

Paige looked between us in shock, obviously understanding this meant something to Brynn. "What? What do you mean she's his sister?"

"Which one?" Brynn asked. Her voice was quiet, almost timid. It unnerved me. Brynn was many things, but never timid. "Which one, Declan? Cami or Elsa?"

"It's Elsa. She's C24."

She bent over, clutched her stomach as if she were in pain, and murmured, "This could break him."

"Brynn?" Paige asked, her voice full of concern.

Brynn rose slowly, then turned to face her. "When Asher was a boy, the Colony took his whole family. They killed his parents, and we always assumed soldiers took both sisters to harvest centers. He was the only survivor, and that's when he came to live with my family. He's blamed himself for his sisters' deaths his entire life."

"And now he's learned one of his sisters is alive. Raised by Silas, who turned her into an assassin for the Colony." Paige shook her head slowly. "I can't imagine how he must feel."

"She was only four-years-old when Asher last saw her. Elsa would be fifteen now. At least he's not alone. He has his sister back." After the broken expression only moments ago, there was now a flicker of hope in her eyes. She believed it would thrill Elsa to be reunited with her big brother.

I had to tell her the truth. No spreading the joy on my part today.

"I really wish it played out that way, but Elsa wants nothing to do with him. She blames Asher for what happened to her and for Cami's death. Said they weren't family and never were."

Brynn froze. If I touched her, I honestly believed she'd shatter or topple over.

"He must be devastated," she whispered.

Paige stood between Brynn and me, arms crossed. "Thinking he needed to work for Silas to keep his family safe, and then finding his sister alive only to lose her again? No wonder he gave control to A36." She narrowed her eyes and took a deep breath.

I felt the full weight of this moment. Either they trusted me and welcomed my help, or left me out in the cold to plot against Silas on my own.

"I never expected to see you again, Declan—hoped, really. Putting my trust in you goes against every instinct in my body. I'm placing my faith in Anna and Asher and their belief in you." Stepping forward, Paige stopped only inches from my face, skepticism flashing in her green eyes. "But if you cross us again, you won't need to worry about A36. I'll end you myself."

9

DECLAN

"The Colony is overpopulated. With the average life span expanded by decades, especially after instituting gene stripping, we've simply run out of room within our gates. We're bursting at the seams." Silas stood at the head of the conference table in his office as he addressed me, Colonel Ackerman, and his advisors. I knew he'd been turning something over in his mind the past several days. Something had distracted him during our meetings, even when I'd updated him on A36's mission outcomes. I knew better than to ask him about it. Since I'd been working so closely with him, I'd learned he preferred to mull over problems on his own, then bestow his glorified solution upon the rest of us inferior mortals. Why he had all these advisors was a mystery. He never sought their advice as far as I could tell. I could only conclude they were his audience because Silas was never happier than when giving a performance.

"To maintain the lifestyle Colony residents have become accustomed to, we need more space. Yes, we could expand into the land outside our gates, but that would take years of planning, building, and demolishing the hovels inhabited by the outliers. As you know, I'm an impatient man." A devilish smile slid across Silas's face as polite laughter drifted around the table. Correction. Terrified laughter. Every one of us knew what would happen if we crossed him. Harvest centers weren't reserved solely for outliers. "As you know, I've been working with Dominic Flores, head of the

Grales territory on adopting our methods of gene stripping in his own region. We've already assisted him in the construction of their first harvest facility. A36 has been instrumental in ensuring the... cooperation of the chosen donors. Thanks to his methods, noncompliance has significantly diminished, although I hear the numbers of orphans and parents without children are on the rise." Silas chuckled.

Ackerman grimaced as I clenched my fists under the table while keeping a fake smile plastered on my face. The Colony made me an orphan. Soldiers ripped my younger twin brothers away from me at a harvest facility. After they deemed my own traits unacceptable and Colony soldiers dumped me in the middle of nowhere, I'd made my way home only to discover an empty house. Judging by the layers of dust and rotten food in the kitchen, my parents had been gone for quite a while. There was no way they'd let the three of us go without a fight, so I'd assumed they'd either gone to look for us or had been taken themselves. After weeks of waiting, I came to the conclusion they weren't coming back. I'd packed up a few belongings, including a picture of the five of us from a camping trip the previous summer, then headed out to join the Insurgents.

"Mr. Flores has generously offered to allow some of our residents to relocate to his territory, which will leave us a more manageable population here in the Colony."

"How will it be determined who moves? By volunteer basis first, then maybe a lottery if we still need to further reduce numbers?" asked Ben, the newest member of the advisory committee.

Those ideas would be shot down. Clearly, he hadn't been here long enough to know Silas and his need for ultimate control. He'd personally choose who was no longer worthy of living behind these gates. I'd only worked closely with the megalomaniac for a few months and had figured that out on day one. Since then, I'd watched Silas chew up and spit out five other advisors. Question his methods, and you're out the door.

"Why would I allow some of our most valuable citizens the choice to leave? Critical decisions such as these can't be left in the hands of those who don't have a firm grasp of the implications of a move. I'll create a list of citizens whose qualifications and contributions are less than ideal, then they'll be notified of their change of residence." Silas glared at Ben with an intensity that radiated around the table, ensuring no other questions would be asked.

"Of course, sir." Under Silas's blistering scrutiny, Ben ducked his head and lowered his gaze. New advisors mistakenly assumed Silas wanted their input. Experienced advisors knew to keep their mouths shut and humor him.

Silas cleared his throat and began again. "Our expansion will require a greater number of donors. As we've depleted desirable outliers within an approximately one-hundred-mile radius, we've had to travel further to find additional sources. Despite our best efforts, Insurgents continue to hamper our efforts and interrupt the supply chain. Our citizens shouldn't be required to wait interminable amounts of time for order fulfillment. After long and careful consideration, I believe I've come up with a solution." He swept his gaze around the table, a superior gleam in his eye, wanting suspense to build before he unveiled his genius plan.

Dread coiled in my stomach.

"We'll continue to recruit donors, but not all of them will be taken to harvest facilities. Based on age, a certain portion will be transferred to breeding centers and housed there for an indefinite period. Males and females will be chosen based on their characteristics. Through in vitro fertilization, their offspring will ensure a steady supply of donors. It's not an immediate solution, but one that will come to fruition within five years."

I fought to maintain an approving smile on my face. Inside I was frozen in horror. Silas was essentially planning baby making factories. Forcing women to carry infants only to turn them over upon their birth to be raised for slaughter. Who does this? What gives Silas the right to decide who lives and dies? Judging by the expressions of the other advisors at the table, they supported his unthinkable plan. Maybe, like me, some of them only pretended to be on board. Disagreement with Silas equaled execution.

"Now that A36 is home, we'll soon move forward with my plan to build an army with his progeny." His face beamed with an almost paternal pride. "Just imagine the talent his children will possess. They'll be unstoppable."

I felt like someone had doused me with ice water. I'm pretty sure I even heard a gasp of shock from Ackerman sitting beside me. This wasn't something he'd previously shared with me or his advisors. Silas wanted to turn Asher's offspring into monsters. They'd receive his enhanced genes but be raised without the family Asher had. Never taught compassion or morals. Never have right from wrong explained to them. Never loved. Silas would ensure they'd become cold, unfeeling killers. Getting Asher out of the Colony was even more critical than I'd believed. And more time-sensitive than ever.

The meeting continued for another hour while Silas performed for his captive audience. After his terrifying reveals, I was on auto pilot, nodding at the appropriate times and struggling to stay present. I'd been answering new advisor Ben's questions when Silas pulled me aside.

"I need to speak with you about a matter of urgency."

"Of course, sir." My immediate thought was that I hadn't schooled my reactions as much as I'd believed, and he'd picked up on my true feelings about his plans. My stomach roiled. I steeled my nerves with the thought that if he'd noticed, he'd have made an example of me during the meeting. Everyone would have seen that no one was exempt from Silas's wrath if they didn't support him. Even his right-hand man.

After the last person exited the room, Silas took his seat to the left of me at the head of the conference table, hands clasped on the glass surface in front of him. "Dominic Flores and his family need to have an unfortunate accident."

This was unexpected. I tilted my head in question. "Sir? I thought our plans were progressing peacefully, and he was embracing the changes. He's even offered space for some of our citizens to relocate."

"Yes, the project is on schedule, and I'm pleased with the progress. A36 has done a marvelous job, and the harvest sites have been busy processing donors." Silas waved his hand dismissively. "The issue is that I can't allow Flores to remain in a position of power. He's an ambitious man, and it's only a matter of time before he makes a move against me. He'll want to control both Grales and the Colony, and I can't allow that to happen. Once he and his family are disposed of, I'll step in and propose overseeing the continuing transformations in their area. We'll make offers to his governing board and military to join our own, then decide what to do with those who don't adapt to the changes quite as easily."

Silas didn't play well with others, so I should have seen this coming. He insisted on being the only rooster in the hen house. I hadn't met Dominic Flores personally, but I knew he had a beautiful wife and three young children. Silas wanted to kill all of them due to the mere possibility Flores might want to wrestle control away from him. Something that wasn't even confirmed. As Flores was sending his own citizens to harvest centers, it wasn't like he had a conscience, but that wasn't the fault of his family. They didn't deserve to suffer because the man was stupid enough to drink Silas's Kool-Aid.

"Did you have something specific in mind?"

"This assignment is top priority and needs to go to someone I trust implicitly. I don't want to pull A36 away from his current mission. Give it to C24. Elsa won't leave any loose ends, and nothing will be traced back to me."

"I'll inform her. She's due in this evening." Elsa would take care of it all right. She lived and breathed for Silas's approval. Talk about a daddy complex. That girl was a textbook example. Even though it was part of my job, spending time with Elsa was at the top of my list of things I'd rather poke needles in my eyes than do. Being raised by Silas for most of her life, she'd always acted as if it was beneath her to have to deal with me on her assignments. Then there was the way she'd treated Asher. I hadn't known about his sisters before coming here, but Elsa made sure everyone knew how he'd abandoned her and Cami when they were younger. Taking A36's actions into account, no one found it difficult to believe. A pack animal he certainly wasn't. I thought there was more to the story. How much could you really remember when you were only four years old at the time? She didn't even give him a chance. But she defended Silas, who was ultimately responsible for the demise of her parents and sister? Just how warped was her brain after spending so much time with him? Wouldn't surprise me at all if she could never be rehabilitated. Some people were just decayed all the way to their core.

•   •   •   •   •

I hung my head in my hands and pulled my hair at the roots. Being tortured by Everly was easier than this. And far less painful. "For the love of all that's holy, just answer my question." Protocol for the agents was to debrief with me in my office within six hours of returning from the field. Compliance would have been one hundred percent across the board if not for one rotten apple.

And I was glaring at her.

Elsa slouched in a chair across the desk from me picking at her fingernails while she dodged and generally ignored my inquiries. Dragging out this process seemed to make her happy, probably because she knew how exasperated and borderline murderous it made me. She challenged my authority at every turn, and not a debrief went by when I didn't imagine wrapping my hands around her throat and squeezing every ounce of life from her. Some days it was a close contest between who I wanted to kill more—her or Silas.

I clenched my fists. Must. Maintain. Control. "Do you enjoy antagonizing people, Elsa? You do it so often, making me repeat protocol to you after every mission, that you must get some freakish kind of pleasure from it."

She sighed heavily and rolled her eyes. I hoped they got stuck that way. "Fine. I terminated the target, and then slipped out through the kitchen staff entrance at 0300 hours."

I gritted my teeth and made a final note in the case file. If only we were finished. Then I could boot her out of my office. Literally. Right now, nothing would give me greater pleasure. Unfortunately, I had orders to pass on. The booting would have to wait. "Silas has a special assignment he wants you to handle personally."

"If he wants me to handle it personally, why doesn't he tell me himself?" She'd recommenced the obsession with her fingernails.

I leveled my gaze at her and cocked an eyebrow. Did we really have to go through this again? My silence was her answer.

She huffed. "Fine. Just tell me what it is so I can get out of here and stop witnessing your power trip. I'm so over it."

"Getting you away from me is the best idea you've had yet. My day would improve tremendously." I sent the file to her data pad.

She made no move to look at the information. Whatever.

"Your targets are Dominic Flores and his family."

She stopped picking at her fingernails and froze. That got her attention. Sitting straight in her chair, she opened the file.

"Silas wants to take out Flores? For what reason?"

"He thinks Flores will make a power move, and he can't have that. You're the only one he trusts to do the job."

Her mouth twisted into a sneer. "What about A36? This seems like a job he'd get a thrill out of."

"Silas wants to keep him focused on his current mission."

She looked to the side and paused a long moment as if turning something over in her mind. "Why the family? He has young children."

"If Flores is the sole victim of an accident, it could look suspicious. With the whole family involved, people are more likely to believe it."

Elsa sat quietly as she looked over the file, a frown on her face. Was she reluctant to take on this assignment? Usually she volunteered for extra missions, and with Silas personally requesting her, I thought she'd pounce on the chance to earn his paternal approval. "Is there a problem, C24?"

Her eyes snapped back to mine. "No. Consider it done."

"Report back to me when it's finished."

"Don't I always?"

"Under penalty of death."

"Do I have permission to leave now?" she asked. Sarcastically, I should add.

"Nothing would make me happier. Don't let the door hit your—" She made a vulgar gesture with her hand, then slammed the door behind her before I could finish my statement. Like I said, some days it was a tie between who I'd like to kill most.

10

BRYNN

Given I was plotting against Silas, worried about Asher, and forever trying to slap some sense into Noah, mounting hostage rescue missions were welcome and much needed distractions for me. Intentionally being in life threatening situations doesn't make the top ten list of stress relievers for most people, but I thrived on it. And if I got to take out my frustrations on a Colony guard who got in the way? Just icing on the cake.

With Paige still acting as interim Controller because of my idiot brother's refusal to end his pity party, she'd assigned me to Luciana's team. Losing Jonah and Jada during Declan's infamous attack on our old compound had devastated Luci. We'd all lost friends and team members, but a proper mourning period had to be put on hold. Finding a new facility, regrouping, recruiting, and training took precedence. The losses fueled even more hatred for the Colony and made us more determined to conquer them. Once that war was over, we'd hold a memorial service for our fallen friends.

Declan's direct involvement had also made him the most likely face to be pinned to a dart board. And trust me, there was no shortage of them at our new place. I'd overheard muttered curses against him with language that would shock even his ears. His alliance with us had to be kept between Paige, Noah, Mom, and me unless we wanted a mutiny on our hands. The fewer people who knew, the safer his secret was. If word of his treason leaked to Silas, our best chance at finally destroying him would disappear and we'd find Declan's body, or what was left of it, on our doorstep.

"ETA ten minutes. Check your gear," Luci instructed.

Mason ran through the standard pre-mission equipment check one last time. I was lucky to have him as a partner. He was experienced in the field and had been on a supply run with Declan, Oz at the time, when Oz had been captured by the Colony. After receiving confirmation from our informant, Aries 7, confirming Oz's death, which was obviously incorrect, Mason had been the one to deliver the news to us while we were gathered in the conference room planning Oz's rescue. Mason had recently been named as head of his own team but was filling in tonight.

Naira was the newest addition, and Luci had taken her under her wing, training extra hours with her. I understood her motives. The potential was there for her to become a strong Insurgent and lead her own team someday. But I hoped with every fiber of my being that day would never come, that our efforts wouldn't be in vain, and the Colony would fall.

Tonight's mission objective was to rescue hostages at a facility closer to the Colony. It was unfamiliar territory for us, but Declan's intel said the conditions were deplorable, and the most recent group of hostages were primarily children. All hostage lives were important, but he and Paige had always had a particular soft spot for children, so she'd made this one a top priority. With three experienced Insurgents on this team and a backup squad just as qualified, our confidence level was high. The transport vans were parked on a dirt road off the main highway a mile from the facility.

"Comm check," Elijah called out. At our old compound, Elijah had begged Noah for months to transfer him to field operative. Elijah was a gifted tech, the best we'd ever had and was told he wasn't cut out for the field. He didn't possess the instincts. I admired the kid's determination because he didn't slink off with his tail between his legs. Instead, he convinced Ash to spend extra time training him. That training paid off when the Colony attacked our compound. Elijah took out a soldier who was seconds away from killing me. After the compound had fallen, Elijah gladly rescinded his request to be a field op. It wasn't the glorious job he'd imagined, and he knew where he could make the biggest contribution to the Insurgents. Still, I was eternally indebted to him.

After completing weapons and comm checks, the eight of us slipped outside the van door and into the darkness. Beta team would remain hidden closer to the facility unless we ran into trouble and needed backup.

"Radio silence until we get there unless it's an emergency," Luci said.

We jogged through the trees under the light of the moon on another hostage rescue mission. After performing what felt like hundreds of missions like this with Ash, I had a flash of déjà vu. A pang of something close to home sickness. Before Declan spazzed out on us and he was still Oz, he, Paige, Asher, and I had been together as a team for so long we'd barely needed to speak during rescues. Most of our communication was nonverbal, and we'd anticipated each other's actions and moves. I'd always had issues with Oz personally, but he never failed to have my back in the field. Luci, Mason, and Naira were just as competent, but it was... different.

Luci slowed and held up her fist for us to stop. We halted at the edge of the tree line facing the fence surrounding the facility, crouched in the high grass. Mason pulled his night vision binoculars from his bag then scanned the area.

Lucy spoke into her comm unit. "How's it look, Elijah?"

"You're cleared to approach," he replied.

Mason nodded in agreement as he stashed the binoculars.

When Declan visited this harvest center earlier today, he'd made sure the security camera covering this particular area was out. I hated to admit it but having him on the inside made our jobs much easier. Not that anyone else on the team knew he was our source. Knowing he interacted with Ash regularly allowed me to maintain a shred of sanity. At least someone who cared about him was close and could give me regular reports. But I'd never admit that to Declan.

This fence wasn't electrified, so we had no problem cutting through the links to slip through. Four buildings stood inside the fence, but we knew the hostages were housed in the largest building at the back of the property. Our intel from Declan indicated two guards were inside with the hostages, and four more were in the building in front of it that contained the cameras, tech area, and a few offices. That was our first target, but to get to it, we had to pass the harvest center first.

Sticking to the shadows of the two-story harvest building, we jogged over the concrete surface. Even now after so many missions, I still shuddered to think about the atrocities that went on in there. Although quiet now, I imagined the cries of fear, pain, and suffering that fell on uncaring ears. Maybe they even lingered sometimes in the dead of night.

With two entrances to the guard building, we split up. Luci motioned she and Naira would take the front, while Mason and I went around back to ensure no one would make a run for it.

"In position," Mason whispered into his comm.

"On the count of three," Luci said. "One, two, ..."

Mason turned the knob. The door swung open quietly. People were so trusting. Idiots. Gun raised, I entered the building first, stepping into a short hallway. Our intel showed this corridor contained a break room and restrooms. I moved swiftly into the break room on my right. My sudden appearance took the guard by surprise. In his haste to stand, he knocked over his chair, and the remains of a half-eaten meal scattered on the table in front of him. He reached for his side arm, but I was faster. Before he could draw, I took aim and shot him in the chest. He staggered backward into the wall, and then slumped to the floor.

Mason met me in the hallway, giving a thumbs up after eliminating another guard in the restroom. I spoke into my comm. "All clear."

Luci replied. "Clear on our end. Proceed to the hostage barracks. Elijah, are we good?"

"Affirmative."

Only two guards left with the hostages. Once we dealt with them, we'd call in the transport vans and get these kids to the compound before being transferred to a safe house. Some days I really loved my job.

When we were halfway across the concrete lot to the barracks, Elijah's voice crackled over our comms. "Paige called an abort, Luci! Immediate abort!"

The four of us halted abruptly. Naira, Mason, and I looked to Luci in confusion. "Elijah, confirm you said abort?"

"Confirm abort. A36 is inbound, only minutes away. Get out now!"

I froze as if ice had been dumped down the back of my shirt. Yet my heart thumped faster—not in fear of him, but in excitement that he was near. No, I reminded myself, A36 was near. Not Asher. Three sets of fearful eyes and shocked faces locked on me. If we were still here when he arrived, he'd slaughter every one of us.

Check that. Not all of us. In my heart, I still didn't believe he could ever hurt me, but I didn't want to test that theory tonight and endanger the others.

Luci gestured with her rifle toward the fence where we'd come in. "Go!" Nairi and Mason sprinted toward our exit point while Luci and I brought up the rear. We had only minutes, maybe less, to make it back across the expansive concrete lot before A36 arrived.

The low growl of a motor reverberated through the night. I glanced over my shoulder to see headlights bobbing in the distance. He was close. Too close. By the whine of the engine, I knew he'd sped up. How had he even seen us? Then I remembered. Damn his enhanced eyesight. We'd never make it to the fence in time.

Light splashed over the four of us as he drew closer.

"Faster!" Luci yelled.

A deafening crash caused me to stop and turn. He'd driven the Jeep through the front entrance. Both gates flipped over top of the vehicle as he skidded to a stop about thirty yards away.

"Keep going! Brynn and I will hold him off until you're clear," Luci said, breathless from running, fear, or both. "Cover us once you're out."

Mason and Naira raced on, while Luciana and I took cover around the corner of the guard house. I chanced a quick peek and saw the Jeep door swing open. A36 crouched behind it with his gun raised, pointed in my direction. I whipped back just as he fired. Brick shards sprayed against my face when his shot hit only inches away.

His eyesight was superior to ours, and I knew he didn't need the headlights to see us. I was surprised he'd left them on. The second the thought crossed my mind, the light disappeared, leaving the glow of the full moon as our only source of light. We carried flashlights, but we'd be idiots to use them. We might as well have hung SHOOT ME signs on our backs.

Shots rang out to my right in the direction Mason and Naira ran. Mason yelped in pain but continued running, favoring his right leg. It wasn't a fatal shot. Not yet anyway. I frowned. That was two times he'd missed the kill shot. Two opportunities to take out half our team.

A36 didn't miss.

Moving targets were nothing to him. Mason had been a dead man running. When he fired at me, the shot went high. What was going on?

A36 shot again, and Naira fell to the ground. It wasn't because she'd stumbled. Mason stopped and bent down, draping her arm over his shoulder. He pulled her up, and they kept moving.

Again, A36 let them go.

I pushed Luci behind me. "Go help them while I distract him. Get them out."

"I'm not leaving you here alone," she hissed.

"He won't hurt me. I know it. Go!"

Luci gawked at me as if I were delusional before she turned and sprinted toward Mason and Naira. I laid down a spray of bullets in front of A36, and he diverted his attention toward me. From the corner of my eye, I saw my three team members move in the direction of the fence. They were easy targets. He could probably pick them off blindfolded based on sound alone.

A36 cast a glance in their direction, and I put a bullet on the ground in front of him to remind him I was still here. Keeping his gun trained on me, he stepped out from behind the shelter of the Jeep door and flashed me a wide smile. A smile I knew well. One that lit up my world and made even the worst of days a little brighter. Only it wasn't quite Asher's smile. This one was laced with malice and challenge. It taunted me, dared me to take the shot. A36 slid through the moonlight quietly like the predator he was, all hard angles and taut muscles. Gone were the sandy blond waves he'd always tied back for mission, his hair now closely cropped.

My hands trembled as I kept him in my sights. What was I doing? A lethal killer closed the distance between us every second, and I stood here waiting for what? A tearful reunion? No matter the certainty I felt deep down that he wouldn't harm me, was I really willing to take that chance? I could be dead in the next thirty seconds.

He was only fifteen feet away now, gun still raised, while I remained cloaked in the building's shadow. "You're not even making this a challenge. Where's the fun in that?" he taunted. Ten feet away.

I'd seen A36 in action back at the Colony when Asher had still been in control. He'd dealt with obstacles quickly and efficiently, then moved on to the next. Teasing the prey wasn't his style. Engaging with the enemy was a waste of time to him. So why was he doing it now?

I stepped away from the shadows and into the moonlight in full view of him. I held up my hands in surrender. "Here I am. You caught me."

He grinned as if this gave him great pleasure. There wasn't even a hint of recognition in his eyes or any sign A36 knew my identity. I was a stranger to him.

"Why didn't you escape with your friends?" he asked.

This was the closest we'd been in months, and I had to restrain myself from going to him. This wasn't my Asher. "Why did you let my team escape? They were easy targets. You don't miss."

A brief expression of confusion flashed across his face as if he didn't quite understand his own actions. "I wounded two of them. That's enough to slow them down."

"Your objective is to wound Insurgents, not kill them? Are those Silas's orders?"

His grin melted away. The corner of his eye twitched.

"What are your orders regarding Insurgents, A36?"

His voice was flat, emotionless. "To eliminate any Insurgents I encounter."

"So why did you allow those three to leave? Why am I still breathing?"

His forearm muscles spasmed, and the gun in his hand quivered.

My questions clearly made him uncomfortable. I forced his mind to places he didn't want to explore.

He blinked hard and inhaled deeply. A bead of sweat trailed down the side of his face. "I didn't... I'll..." He brought up his other hand and gripped the gun so tightly his knuckles whitened.

I moved a step closer, tempting him, almost begging him to pull the trigger. His brows drew together in confusion.

"Why aren't you following orders? What's keeping you from killing me?"

Tremors wracked his body, and he squeezed his eyes shut. His jaw tightened. Yet he kept his weapon trained on me. The thought crossed my mind that his quivering hands could accidentally pull the trigger, and he could end my life whether he'd intended it or not. Whatever he grappled with was powerful enough to prevent him from obeying Silas's orders.

His eyes popped open. They were tortured. And intimately recognizable. "Brynn... go. Please."

Asher.

His voice was coarse and strained, but achingly familiar. "I can't hold... Run."

I fled.

He didn't come after me. Somehow Asher had prevented A36 from chasing me down. He'd also kept him from hurting our team. Not badly anyway. Mason and Naira had suffered only superficial leg wounds, nothing close to life-threatening.

Paige shook her head. "I don't understand how the four of you are still alive. How is this possible?"

I sat across from her in her office during the debriefing. Luci was checking on Naira and Mason while medical tended to their wounds. Saying the three of them, the beta team, and Elijah were shocked to see me climb into the van was putting it mildly. They'd been strategizing with beta team on how they'd get me out without losing everyone, especially since two of them were already wounded.

Paige was usually a low-key, keep emotions bottled up inside, don't-let-them-see-you-sweat kind of girl, but our survival had truly astonished her, and her face showed it.

After I ran, I didn't take time to check in with Luci or Elijah, not that I could have spared the extra oxygen. Ash had struggled hard enough to give me a window to escape. I wasn't wasting it.

I'd been right all along. Having me stand before him, an Insurgent he'd been ordered to eliminate on sight, had been the ultimate test. And Asher had passed. Killing me wasn't something he was capable of, even as his alter-ego killing machine. Despite A36's lack of recognition, deep down inside whatever cavern he was trapped in, Ash knew it was me. He'd also sensed Luci and Mason were friends. He'd never met Naira but deemed her a friend since she'd been with us.

Asher was still in there, and he was fighting.

"Why was he there? Declan said we were clear. Is that worm no longer reliable?"

"No, the intel was good, but A36 took off on his own without Declan knowing. Why is anyone's guess, but we're lucky Declan questioned his absence and there was a GPS tracker on his vehicle." The set of Paige's jaw was grim. As was her tone. "He could have killed you, Brynn. What possessed you to put yourself in his path like that? There's no way you could have known the outcome."

I debated telling her this because it was deeply personal and something only Asher and I had discussed. Betraying his trust was the last thing I'd ever do, and respecting each other's privacy was built into the foundation of our relationship. All things considered, Paige was my Controller and had a right to know information that could affect us in the field. But more than that, she was our friend, and I didn't think Ash would mind if I shared this with her. "When Asher first discovered what he was, he wanted to leave because he believed he'd hurt me. He had this recurring dream about waking up in our bed covered in my blood, my body lying cold beside him. I reassured him over and over that would never happen. He became A36 to protect his family and at his core, that will always be his biggest need. Even A36 can't override Ash's love for his family. I was right."

Paige nodded, but I could tell she was still skeptical. "It was really Asher just for those few moments? You're sure?"

I smiled and clung tightly to the tingling warmth I felt inside from being with him for the barest of moments. "Positive. It was him." He'd fought with everything he had to protect me. Even though our time together was brief, it proved something I'd been wrestling with in my mind. Something that could help us get things back on the track to winning this war. "This gives me an idea."

Paige tilted her head to the side. "Spill it. You may have to speak slowly. My mind is still recovering from the shock that you're all safe."

If my plan worked, this could be the last piece we needed to defeat Silas. Asher had been strong enough to push A36 aside for a few moments. It was a gamble, but I had to believe he'd be capable of locking him up for good. If I could draw him out long enough to let him know the trackers were gone, he could fight A36. And I was confident he'd win. He could rejoin us and stop A36's reign of terror. "We'll need Declan."

DECLAN

Silas was in some kind of mood tonight, tossing around his authority and playing Lord of the Manor to the hilt. Even though we'd met just hours earlier, he'd demanded my immediate presence to discuss some mystery topic. In the wee hours of the morning. Not that he'd woken me. With all my covert maneuverings, the high probability of failure to take down Silas, and my double life, my mind shunned rest and preferred to keep spinning hour after hour, night after night. Sleep was about as likely as me surviving the next three months. Even my ill-gotten genetic enhancements couldn't hide the dark circles beneath my eyes. Studies had been done about how long people could go without sleep and still have the capability to make rational choices or even function. Maybe I should look up those results before I keeled over or started making stupid decisions. Or stupider that those I'd already made. Would I even be able to tell the difference?

The elevator door opened silently to the foyer outside Silas's private quarters. I'd been here before, but the extravagance never failed to repulse me. Because of the Colony, there were adults and children out there trying to pick up the pieces of their shattered lives and regain some sense of normalcy, while Silas sat in his perfect castle doling out fates to people like a dealer in a poker game.

One of the two guards stationed at either side of the door opened it to allow me entry, then closed it behind me. Unlike his office, Silas's private quarters were decorated more traditionally. Warmer tones of rich chocolates, deep reds, and earthy moss. Chairs that hugged you when you sank into them. Low lights that gave a more intimate feel. Even a fireplace to drive away the chill. Almost like a real person lived here instead of a hollow, unfeeling megalomaniac.

Tonight, only the dancing flames in the fireplace and the golden light of a table lamp beside Silas lit the room. He sat in his favorite leather armchair in front of the fire, a glass of dark liquid in his hand. Probably bourbon. He had a strong preference for it, but rarely allowed himself the indulgence.

"Declan, is that you?"

Judging by his slurred words, he'd allowed himself to over-imbibe tonight. "Yes, sir." My shoes sank into the plush carpet as I approached the fireplace where he could see me. I halted abruptly. His appearance had never been anything less than perfect, but now his clothes were disheveled, and his hair looked like a family of squirrels had taken up residence. I doubted many people had ever seen him like this, if any. It was completely out of character for him.

It also made me wonder what had transpired that he allowed himself to be in this state.

He dragged his gaze up to me with unfocused eyes and heavily patted the arm of the chair next to him. "Have a seat."

Although I couldn't show it, I was completely unnerved. The steely-eyed, calculating, soul-stealing serpent had been replaced with a bourbon-guzzling lush. He was utterly defenseless and if it weren't for the constant camera surveillance and guards outside the door, I'd take full advantage of this opportunity and end him right now.

But someone else would take his place, and we'd be back to square one.

Patience was required to do this the right way, no matter how I felt. Keep the end goal in sight. Let Silas guide the conversation and see what I could find out while listening to his drunken prose.

I lowered myself into the chair. "Did you want to discuss something, sir?"

He waved a hand dismissively while lifting his glass to his lips and taking a long drink. After swallowing hard, it took him a couple of tries to set the empty glass back on the table. "When does Elsa return from her mission? I miss her."

"She came in two days ago and started prepping for the next one."

His brows drew together in confusion. "She's back? But... why hasn't she been here?"

"I don't know, sir. Maybe she's busy getting ready for the next assignment."

Silas picked up his empty glass and tried to stand but fell heavily back to his chair.

"Let me get that for you." I carried his glass to the lavishly stocked bar, top shelf liquors only, in the corner and poured a generous amount into the tumbler. I needed to keep him talking before he passed out cold. Something wasn't right, and for whatever reason, he'd asked me here to keep him company. It wasn't like Silas had any friends or a tribe he hung out with. He surrounded himself with people who supported his views and policies predominantly out of fear for their lives.

I set his drink on the table then returned to my chair.

"Thank you, you're a good boy." He took another long sip while gazing into the fire. "Do you have family, Declan?"

His words were like a slap in the face. *No, you killed my twin brothers, and I have no idea what happened to my parents, you son of a...* "I'm alone, sir. I've been on my own for quite a while."

He nodded slowly. "Elsa is my only family. I raised her from the age of four. Did you know that?"

Is that what this was about? Family? What the hell made him think after everything and everyone he'd destroyed that he deserved love of any kind? After having Elsa's parents killed, he'd made her an orphan then spent the last decade hunting down her brother. "I knew you and Elsa were close, but I didn't know you'd raised her." He was well down the road to drunk town if he thought I was unaware of what he'd done.

"She's like a daughter to me, you know. Her father was employed by me years ago, but things didn't... work out for him, and he could no longer care for her. She was a beautiful child, and I offered her a home here with me."

I wondered if I should move to another chair because surely the gates of Hell would open up and swallow him whole for the lies he told. I didn't want to get sucked up in the wake. "That was very generous of you. Elsa was a lucky girl." Maybe I'd go with him for the lies that rolled off my tongue.

"She moved in with me but was very shy at first. I already had a bedroom perfect for a young girl and told her if there was anything else she wanted, she only needed to ask."

Already had a bedroom ready for a young girl? I shuddered in horror at the implications of what that statement could mean. If he gave any indication that he'd taken advantage of Elsa and hurt her, screw the plan. I'd kill him with my bare hands right now.

"She warmed up to me after a while and we became a family, just the two of us. Such a loving child." He chuckled. "But so clumsy. Elsa could barely walk across a flat surface without stumbling over her own feet. Falls and bruises were a daily occurrence with her. Fortunately, we corrected those flaws. And just look at her now." He beamed, parental pride written all over his abnormally smooth face. And those "flaws" were corrected by stripping genes from people who were guilty of nothing more than being born with outstanding balance.

His earlier comment about having a bedroom ready for a young girl made me more curious than a cat. I almost dreaded the answer, but the question begged to be asked. "Sir, if I may ask, what did you mean when you said a bedroom for a young girl was already made up? Was there someone else here before Elsa?"

Silas side-eyed me, then his gaze returned to the fire, light dancing in those cold, dark eyes of his. What was this? His eyes shimmered... with tears? Sadness was too human an emotion for him. Surely he wasn't capable of experiencing it. Silas only cared about himself and Elsa. Or so I'd thought. This night might lead to some shocking revelations.

He took a long sip of his drink, then tried to set it on the table again. It nearly slid off twice before finding purchase. I silently begged him not to pass out before answering my questions. "There was," he said, almost whispering. "Years ago, I had a wife and daughter. It was just the three of us that lived here. My wife, Marilee, was a beautiful woman. Luckily, she'd inherited her mother's genes, because her father wasn't much to look at, and they didn't have the resources to change that." He grimaced as if it was painful to even remember someone who was physically unattractive and poor. "Growing up in poverty, she wanted more out of life. A better life. And I could offer her that.

"We married within months after we met. She took to this life as if she'd been born to it. Being in my position required meeting with and entertaining dignitaries from other territories. She became well-versed on their backgrounds and knew the perfect things to say. A gracious hostess every time, and a true asset to my career."

I couldn't imagine Silas having a wife. Caring about someone enough to marry her. But by the way he spoke of her—beautiful and an asset to his career—I doubted love was any part of the equation. Sounded more like a business deal to me. He provided the financial security she'd lacked growing up, and she maintained the illusion of an adoring wife who supported him in every way.

"Before long, she wanted a child to complete our family. Someone to add to our already perfect lives. I knew our child would be flawless—stunning, intelligent, and exceptional." Silas's mouth twisted into a drunken scowl. "And she was. Intelligent, that is. Off the charts, in fact. Unfortunately, Sabine had inherited her maternal grandfather's rather bland features. Limp, mousy hair. Short stature. Like Elsa, not the most graceful creature to stumble around the Colony. Other than her intelligence, she was an overall disappointment."

I counted myself lucky to be sitting, because I surely would have keeled over if I'd been standing when he dropped that bombshell. Not only did Silas have a wife, but a daughter, too? And to describe her that way—an overall disappointment—because she didn't live up to his physical expectations? There were people in this world who'd give anything to be blessed with a healthy child. Thousands of them had, only to lose them to harvest facilities. Our neighbors beside the house I grew up in had wanted children for years but were unable to have any. They often told my parents how fortunate they were to have three sons. Yet, scum like Silas became a father and spoke of his child with such disregard. It was shameful. Sinful. Deplorable.

"We kept her out of the public eye, but when she neared the age of four, I was ready to have her features enhanced. Make her into the child we should have had. Marilee wouldn't hear of it and initially refused, but I made it clear it wasn't negotiable. As the leader of the Colony, I couldn't be seen with such an average child. I had a certain image to maintain, and perfection was happiness. Mediocrity was unacceptable." Even now he looked as if it pained him to discuss his daughter's imperfections.

Parents were supposed to love their children unconditionally, which just added support to my opinion that Silas should never have been blessed with a child.

"She reluctantly agreed," he continued, "and the procedures were carried out successfully. Sabine was perfect in every way and would make any parent proud. She was a very curious child and constantly asked questions about her world." He lifted his glass to his lips and spilled some of the bourbon before it met his mouth, eyes growing even more unfocused as he reminisced.

"We were happy for several years, but I should have seen it coming. Sabine began asking questions about our way of life. She wanted to know about the people outside the gates, what their lives were like. Why her nanny had brown eyes one week and violet the next. She found old photos of herself from before the enhancements and asked if she'd had a sister. I explained the flaws she'd been born with and procedures she'd undergone to correct her shortcomings. Sabine was furious and couldn't understand why she'd never been good enough for us, why we couldn't have loved her for what she was. Why others died so she could look the way she did. Soon after, we woke one morning, and she was gone. Our daughter left us, and I haven't seen her since then. I have no idea what became of her."

An icy hand gripped my heart. Silas's story about his daughter was familiar in a disturbing way. Remarkably familiar. I needed more information. I had to know if my suspicions were correct. If they were, my life just became a lot more complicated.

"Silas?" His chin rested on his chest, and his eyelids drooped. I needed to keep him awake just a little longer. "I'm sorry your daughter didn't appreciate everything you'd done for her. I can't imagine the pain you and your wife went through after losing her."

"Marilee...killed herself..." he mumbled. His wife committed suicide? If she'd fought against the surgery for their daughter, I could see how she might blame Silas for what happened. Maybe even herself for not standing up to him. It surprised me this was the first I'd heard of Silas having a wife who died and a daughter who ran away. Knowing his desire for perfection, he'd probably created a plausible story that kept all the ugliness hidden, even though he'd been responsible for all of it. His quest for perfection had driven away the very people he seemed to have cared about.

"I'd love to see a picture of your daughter. Do you have any here?" Silence, other than the sound of his heavy breathing and light snoring. He was out cold. Which provided me a golden opportunity. Now I was free to roam around his apartment in search of a family photo. Who knew what other interesting tidbits I might discover?

Two framed photos sat on the fireplace mantel in front of me. I rose from the chair and examined them. One was of Silas with two other couples on a yacht. The other was of him and a woman I assumed was Marilee. He hadn't been exaggerating. She was stunning. I set the pictures back on the mantel and wandered into the impeccable kitchen. Nothing but sterile white counters and lots of stainless steel. Maybe his bedroom? Ducking back into the living room for a quick peek, I made sure he was still out. His chest rose and fell steadily.

Two exits led from the living area, one on either side of the room. I chose left first and counted four closed doors along the hallway. Taking one last glance over my shoulder, I crept silently toward the first one. I opened the door and flicked on the light. Bed, nightstand, a small sitting area—looked like an unused guest room. My eyes darted across the furniture, but no photos were displayed here. The next two rooms were similar. That left only one more, which had to be Sabine's room, Elsa's more recently. I halfway expected it to be locked, but the knob turned easily, and I slowly swung the door open.

I switched on the light and was immediately assaulted by an explosion of pink. Light pink, fuchsia, neon—every shade on the pink color wheel. It was nearly blinding. Thinking of Elsa, a tough as nails, stone cold killer in this room, my lips twisted into a smirk, and I covered my mouth to avoid laughing out loud. It looked more like a room for an eight-year-old. No wonder she'd moved out at such a young age. I'd love to tease her about this, but she could never know I had seen it. Besides, any taunts from me would only encourage her to hate me even more than she already did.

I examined the few framed photos that sat on a bookshelf filled with children's books, but they were of Elsa when she was younger or her and Silas together. Another dead end. Closing the door behind me, I rubbed my eyes. I still saw pink behind my eyelids. How someone could sleep in that room was a mystery to me. It was like living inside a cotton candy machine.

I had one last option. The hallway on the other side of the living area had to lead to Silas's bedroom. There were no other levels in this apartment. He still snored softly as I tread lightly through the room. His neck would probably have a crick in it tomorrow. Good. Thinking about him experiencing even the slightest bit of pain made my day a little brighter.

The short hallway led to two massive double doors made of dark wood. They seemed opulent enough to guard Silas's bedroom. I pushed open the heavy doors to dimly lit quarters. Like the rest of Silas's home, apart from Elsa's room, it was spotless and masculine. No clothes strewn across the floor, no shoes kicked off haphazardly or books stacked on the nightstand waiting to be read.

But there were several framed photos gathered on a draped table in the corner. I swallowed hard and advanced toward it. My peripheral vision narrowed to the point that the table was the only thing I saw. I felt as if I were in a long corridor. The faster I moved, the further away it seemed. Once I reached it, I'd discover if my suspicions were correct. But did I really want to know the truth? It could be a game changer.

I closed my eyes and shook my head to clear it. Silas could wake at any moment, and I couldn't afford to waste time on illusions. I pressed on and stopped a couple feet away from the table. Along with the pictures was a stuffed teddy bear, a gold locket, and a few children's books. It was a shrine to his lost daughter.

I picked up the smallest photo. Silas stood beside Marilee, who held an infant in a pink blanket. Silas hadn't aged a day since then, but it was the undeniable ecstatic smile across his face that threw me. I'd never seen him like this. From all appearances—his somber mood this evening, the shrine, and his expression in the picture—Silas had genuinely loved his daughter. His own version of love, I guess, and as much as he was capable of. The other pictures showed Sabine at various ages. In one, she sat on a swing, a wide smile on her face. She seemed to be a happy little girl, but I remembered what Silas had said about her features being plain and unacceptable for the child of a man in his position.

Anger coursed through my body. After I'd been captured by the Colony years ago, they'd pronounced my features and abilities unacceptable and dumped me at the side of the road with other kids who'd been categorized in the same way. But here was a picture of a beautiful little girl whose parents decided she wasn't good enough through no fault of her own.

That wasn't love.

The next two appeared to be of a different child, but I knew it was still Sabine. She was young in these, maybe around five or six years old. I set down the frame and picked up the largest one at the back of the table. It must have been the last one taken before Sabine left. She stood between Silas and Marilee, arms crossed, and her face scrunched into a frown.

Recognition surged through me like a tidal wave. The floor tilted beneath me, and I grabbed onto the edge of the table to steady myself. Scrunched face or not, I knew who this was. Sabine wasn't a stranger to me.

I dropped the frame and staggered backward as all the air was sucked out of my lungs. Even though she was several years younger, her identity was unmistakable. I'd spent hours observing her when I thought she wasn't looking. Worked side by side with her for years.

Been in love with her.

My hunch had been correct. Paige was Silas's daughter.

12

DECLAN

After helping Silas, who totally reeked of bourbon, over to a sofa and covering him with a blanket, I slipped out and headed to my quarters, still reeling from my discovery. Paige was Silas's daughter. If someone told me Brynn possessed a secret collection of stuffed unicorns, I'd have sooner believed that outlandish notion. I still couldn't wrap my mind around it. Several years together working side by side in the field, numerous stakeouts, just the two of us for hours at a time, fighting a common enemy—who happened to be her father—and she'd never mentioned it. Not a word, not a peep, not a sound.

Paige worked twice as much, and harder than most Insurgents. She volunteered for other missions on downtime, spent hours with rescued children at the compound, and trained new recruits. But no one had ever questioned why. We just thought she had a killer work ethic. All of us were there for a reason, and some people chose not to discuss what brought them to the Insurgents. Maybe it was personal and private, and that choice was respected. Who would have guessed Paige had a wickedly dark, underlying reason? I couldn't blame her, though. I sure as hell wouldn't tell anyone if Silas was my father. Talk about your social pariah.

The day the Colony attacked our compound, when I'd stolen Brynn away from Ash and admitted my feelings to Paige. The day I'd spend the rest of my life trying to make up for, the day Paige said she could never love me and loathed me for what I'd done. She'd spilled what I'd thought was the reason behind her tireless work ethic—and it was the truth. Just not all of it. When she'd been young, and without her consent, her parents had her genetically altered. Years later when she was at an age to understand what this meant, she'd left. I wondered how long she'd been on her own, the amount of courage it must have taken to leave everything familiar and head into the unknown. What a brave young girl she'd been. Didn't surprise me a bit.

When Silas told me the story about his daughter, it rang of familiarity. If I lived to be a thousand years old, I'd never forget what Paige said about her parents. On the surface the stories were remarkably similar, but deep down I'd hoped it wasn't true, prayed it was just a wild coincidence.

When you stopped to think about it, letting the world know your father was a power hungry, narcissistic sociopath wasn't something that came up in casual conversation. Or anything you'd be proud to share. Asher's shock mirrored my own at Paige's admission that day, so if he hadn't known about her being genetically enhanced, it was a safe bet Noah and Brynn knew nothing about her past, either.

From Silas's drunken ramblings, it was clear he still cared about Paige, but had absolutely no idea where she might be. I wondered if he still looked for her or maybe had people trying to track her whereabouts? If so, and if he found her, the new compound could be destroyed just as easily as the last. Silas had no problem with collateral damage as long as it got him what he wanted. I might have been responsible for the destruction of the last one, but I wouldn't let it happen again on my watch if it was preventable.

I needed to meet with Paige.

• • •

A soft breeze blew through the trees overhead as I waited for Paige in the clearing. Leaves in brilliant colors swirled in a lazy descent to the forest floor. Autumn had always been my favorite season when I was younger. Football with my friends, bonfires, campouts with my younger twin brothers in the backyard before the weather grew too cold. I'd give anything to have those simpler days again. To be with my family again.

Dry leaves crunched as Paige emerged from the trees. That she'd agreed to meet me without bringing Brynn proved I was making headway in regaining her trust. Of course, Brynn could snipe me from the trees, finger on the trigger itching to take the shot. But that wasn't her style. If she was going to take me out, nothing less than face to face where she could witness the pain she inflicted up close and personal would satisfy her.

Wind lifted strands of Paige's dark tresses around her head and made me think of Medusa's hair made up of snakes. She stopped several feet away. I got it. She still wasn't completely comfortable with me, but I was determined to win her trust again. "Since you asked me to come without Brynn, either you don't have news about Asher, or you have bad news you don't want her to hear, and you're too afraid to tell her yourself. If that's the case, you know her reaction won't be pleasant when she finds out you withheld information from her."

"It's nothing about Ash." I swallowed hard. "It's about you, Paige." She raised her brows in surprise but gestured for me to continue. A woman who preferred not to waste words. "Silas called me to his apartment late the other night. He'd ingested enough alcohol to inebriate a rhinoceros, and he told me a story."

I only noticed the subtle narrowing of her eyes because I watched closely for a reaction. Did she suspect I'd discovered her secret? "He told me about his beautiful wife and how happy they'd been before she died. About the young girl who lived in Elsa's room years ago. About his daughter and how he and his wife had woken one morning to find her gone after she'd learned about her genetic enhancements." Note to self: Never play poker with this girl. Her face didn't reveal a thing. She had no obvious tells.

"How does this affect me, Declan? Why am I here?"

"After Silas passed out, I took the chance to snoop around the apartment. He'd made a shrine to his daughter in his bedroom. I found the pictures, Paige. I know you're Sabine."

She didn't even flinch, her face an emotionless mask. She stared at me unmoving for what felt like several long minutes but was probably only seconds. Finally, she squared her jaw and spoke in a flat voice. "Yes, I'm his biological daughter."

That's it? That's all she was going to say? "Why didn't you tell someone? Don't you think this is something the Insurgents needed to know?"

She blinked once. "Why would it be important?"

Incredible. Paige wasn't budging an inch. "You're the daughter of Silas, the overlord, the big cheese, maybe even the antichrist!"

Annoyance flickered across her face. "Listen closely, Declan. He may be my biological father, but I haven't considered myself his daughter since the day I learned what he did to me. He made it very clear I hadn't been good enough, that I was an embarrassment. As if my physical appearance was so hideous, society would shun me or think less of him and my mother. Maybe by the Colony's standards, where everyone holds beauty and perfection in the utmost regard and base a person's worth on their appearance. People should never be judged by their outer shell, only on what's inside. What they contribute to the world and how they choose to live. How they love the people in their lives. That's what really counts. My parents should have loved me, not my appearance. No one should have died for me to gain their love and approval. To me, he's empty inside, and nothing but an enemy to be taken down."

Her words hit me like a punch to the gut, proving once again how badly I'd misjudged what was important to her when I'd traded my friends for a new face and body. From the day she'd left home, Paige had worked tirelessly as an Insurgent, worked back-to-back missions, functioned with very little sleep at times, and continually put her life on the line. All to try and correct her father's wrongs. To balance the scale of good and evil. It was only a drop in a roaring river, but she gave all she had. What a strong person she was to be on her own at such a young age and not let her parents' shallow opinions crush her spirit. I wondered if I'd ever meet another person who was as beautiful as Paige—and I didn't mean on the outside.

"I'm so sorry, Paige. Sorry you had to go through that, sorry you lost your mother. I'll never stop apologizing for misjudging you so badly." I sighed heavily. "If it's any consolation, as much as Silas is able to show any sort of emotion, he seems to miss you and love you."

She shook her head. "No. He loves the idea of me, the perfect child he could put on display. Even then, I knew his feelings for me were hollow. Silas only loves himself."

"You certainly have my condolences at having to grow up in a room that looks like a cotton candy machine detonated. Please tell me it wasn't like that when you lived there."

Her mouth quirked into a half smile. "Again, my parents' idea of what a little girl's room should look like." She held her hands out to the side and gestured toward the calf length gray coat over her signature black pants and shirt. "Have you ever seen me wear pink?"

I wrinkled my nose and laughed. "Imagining you in that room was against the laws of nature. Like a chicken being the king of the jungle. He didn't change it when Elsa moved in, and it doesn't suit her any better, trust me."

After today, I thought maybe Paige did just a little more.

13

DECLAN

It was difficult to describe my feelings when I received word Brynn wanted to meet with me. My stomach did a 360-degree flop before sinking to my feet. I was sure her ulterior motive was to kill me for some unknown indiscretion or offense I'd unknowingly committed. I searched my memory for a reason, reviewed every interaction we'd had as well as every piece of intel I'd sent their way to try and figure out what I'd done wrong and came up with nothing. But why else would she want to talk?

From the first day we'd met, Brynn had scrutinized me with an intensity that left me rattled and paranoid. She evaluated my every move, interaction, and reaction in the field as an operative. Hell, my every move between missions, too. That girl never trusted me. Asher reassured me that was just her default setting and was nothing personal. Mostly.

That was before I'd given her every reason to never trust me under any circumstance. Before I'd betrayed the only people who'd felt like family since I'd lost my own. Maybe she'd sensed the darkness lurking just below the surface that would lead me to turn on them.

Whether she believed it or not, I'd changed my stripes. At heart, I'd always be an Insurgent. Even though I risked my own life every day playing a double agent, I knew my actions would never bring back the dead. Everything I did wasn't just for atonement. Destroying the Colony was the right thing to do. If I went down while working against Silas, I'd do everything I could to cut the head off the snake first.

Dead leaves crunched beneath my feet, and a blue autumn sky sliced through the branches above. Sweat sluiced down the middle of my back. Not that it was particularly warm outside or from physical exertion. It was the threat of Brynn. Meeting in the middle of a forest, just the two of us, was her idea. With all these woodland meetings, I briefly wondered if I should just set up another office. I figured this way she could kill me and then hide the body in the same place. Made her job easier and saved time, right? Then she could just go on with her day and check me off her to-do list.

We'd come across this abandoned house during a mission last year when things had gone off the rails, and we hadn't been able to get back to transport. Asher, Brynn, Paige, and I escaped on foot. The four of us had taken out every Colony guard on our trail, but it was the middle of the night, our comms were spotty, and we were just looking for somewhere to hunker down until the light of day. This place offered seclusion and shelter for a few hours, and with windows on every side of the house, we had a 360-degree view if there were any unwelcome surprises.

I climbed the stone steps leading to the porch, then paused and stared at the heavy oak door. I may or may not leave this house again. My fate rested in Brynn's freakishly strong hands. She knew I was here. I could feel her hardened gaze on me, daring me to cross the threshold.

"Are you going to waste my time and stand out there all day or grow a set and come inside?"

I turned the knob and then pushed the door open slowly, its rusty hinges screeching from disuse. Brynn stood in front of the fireplace, long braids draped over her shoulder and arms folded over her chest. I noted the gun still holstered at her side. From years of working together, I also knew she carried a knife in her boot. At least her hands were nowhere near either of them. That was a good sign. But I'd seen how fast she moved, so my relief was fleeting.

"Close the door, Declan. Or did you bring some of your Colony friends for backup?"

After shutting the door, I turned to face her and stumbled over my own feet. Faced with Silas and armed Colony soldiers? Grace under pressure. Alone with Brynn in a room? My mind nearly whited out in terror.

Sometimes I wondered how kind, loving, and good-natured Anna had birthed such a stern, distrustful creature.

"O-of course not."

Brynn arched a brow in doubt as her gaze swept over me, then returned to my face as if searching for signs of deceit.

She wouldn't find any.

"Sit down." Brynn nodded toward a wooden chair with a slat missing from the back.

I moved toward the chair and lowered myself into it, my shaky legs grateful for the reprieve.

She took the battered, floral print sofa across from me. Her unwavering gaze never left my face. "I want to believe I can trust you, Declan, but we really don't need to rehash all the reasons I don't."

My head bobbed in agreement, not wanting to interrupt and risk her wrath.

"Anna believes in you. Paige is leaning in your direction. I'm still not convinced. But I'll admit you've delivered on your promises over the past month." Her mouth drew into a flat line, and she blinked slowly, hesitating with her next words. "If I had other options, I'd take them. Honestly, being in the same room with you requires constant restraint on my part not to hurt you. All the painful ways I could do it constantly flash through my mind." Her lips drew into a dreamy smile as if those thoughts entertained her.

I'd expect no less.

My legs twitched, and adrenaline surged through me. My body begged to use its flight response before Brynn acted on one of those options.

"I need your help."

My heart stuttered in shock. She'd never come to me for anything before. Ever. With her monstrous trust issues, Brynn relied on an abbreviated list of people—only three that I knew of. Now four since Anna was back. Asking for my help cost her a lot. I intended to deliver whatever it was and make sure she didn't regret it. "I want to help. Anything you need, Brynn. I'll do whatever I can."

"I need to see him."

Except that.

I sagged back into my chair and shook my head. She was asking me to sign her death warrant. "You know he's not Asher anymore. A36 governs him and his actions."

"I can reach him. You just need to get me into the Colony."

"Brynn, no. The second you stepped foot inside the gates, Silas would know. He'd find you and probably send A36 to kill you while he enjoyed the show. That would be the ultimate test of his loyalty, killing the person Asher loves most." She didn't realize what she was asking. Brynn had only seen A36 when Asher controlled him, not the calculating predator he was now. When she'd been in A36's presence at the harvest facility, I honestly believed it was some kind of warped amalgam of the two of them. Not fully A36 or Asher.

"Then take me to where he'll be in the field. I know you give out the assignments. I wouldn't need long."

"I don't know if he'd recognize you. Even if he did, I doubt he'd care who you were. People mean nothing to him. A36 is a machine. He eats, kills, sleeps, wakes, and then starts all over again." I sighed heavily. "Yes, I dole out his assignments and see him regularly. But I never turn my back on him. He can't be trusted."

Brynn leaned forward, intent on convincing me. "*I* trust him, and that's all that matters. He didn't hurt me that night at the harvest facility. Asher stopped him. For any of this to work, we need him. You know it."

Putting her in a room with A36 would be the same as shoving her into a pit of starving lions. Sure, I knew we'd eventually need Asher back. It was inevitable. Bringing him home to his family and taking Silas down were my two biggest priorities. I'd hoped by some miracle he'd snap out of it on his own, but it was clear A36 had a steel grip on him. Voluntarily putting anyone else in his path was something I'd tried to avoid, but it might just be necessary. "If I put the two of you together, what happens if he attacks you? Even if I was with you, there's no way the two of us could hold him off. I couldn't live with myself if something happened." I snorted out a laugh. "Guess I wouldn't have to if we were both dead, right?"

"He won't hurt me." Her expression left no doubt she believed that with unwavering certainty. And I wanted to believe it just as much.

I shook my head slowly. "You can't know that. Asher left the building a long time ago."

"He was Asher long enough to warn me to run when A36 interrupted our mission. Before that, he stood only feet away and had every opportunity to take out our team and me. He didn't. Ash prevented him from hurting us."

I ran my hands through my hair. When A36 had gotten bored at the new harvest location in Flores's territory, he'd gone searching for more action. After hearing about the security cameras being out at the facility the Insurgents raided, it must have triggered an alarm inside him. It was a familiar technique Asher would have recognized, so maybe A36 had subconsciously picked up on it. I'd been out of my mind with worry that night, convinced we'd lose the whole team. By some miracle, they'd been spared.

"If you don't help me, you know I'll find a way to get to him myself. It would be a hell of a lot easier if you pitch in." Brynn's resolute expression left no doubt in my mind she'd do exactly that and maybe get herself killed before she even reached A36. Nothing would keep her away from Ash.

Looked like she made my decision for me.

"All right. I'll help. I don't know yet how I'll make it happen, but I promise I'll find a way to get the two of you in the same place." Whatever plan I came up with, it had to be something that didn't trigger A36's warning lights. That was no easy feat. He was like a human lie detector. We'd also have to take precautions to protect ourselves from him in case Brynn couldn't reach Asher. I knew Asher would fight like hell to take back control once he was with Brynn, but it wouldn't be a picnic.

A36 wouldn't go back in storage quietly.

14

DECLAN

As I walked down to the shooting range to meet with A36, my focus was on coming up with some way to divert him from the next mission and get him in the same room with Brynn. All without making him suspicious. If she couldn't pull Asher up from the sunken depths of the vessel he shared with A36, no one could. If she failed, then my goal, my sworn promise of returning Ash to his family, would be unreachable. What A36 might do to us when he realized what was happening was a scenario that fueled my nightmares.

But I was stubborn. Ask anyone who knew me as Oz. Or as Declan now. Stubbornness had helped me survive the frigid nights, near starvation, and cabin fire after Colony soldiers dumped me at the side of the road. It took me back to my home where I waited weeks for my parents before laying them to rest in my mind. Then it carried me to the Insurgents where I could help make a difference in this screwed up world. When the odds were against me and the chips were down, I never gave up.

Okay, taking recent history into consideration, I'd concede maybe I didn't make the best decisions sometimes, but I was under duress and hoped a new genetic panel would achieve my dream of being with Paige. Stupidity wasn't a crime. Poor choices were an unfortunate side effect.

But I digress. I had to keep the goal front and center.

The shooting range was located several hundred yards behind the Tower. It wasn't in the middle of a forest, but there were plenty of trees and shrubs surrounding it to make it aesthetically pleasing. Which was, of course, a priority within these cursed gates. Heaven forbid Colony residents be exposed to any dead trees or straggly bushes. Such disturbing trauma could cause unhappiness, which might lead to frown lines. What a tragedy that would be.

Creatively designed, the open gun range lay at the bottom of a bowl-shaped crater in the earth. It was an expansive facility, and operatives and soldiers were free to come practice at any time. Unless A36 was there. Not that he requested sole use of the range, but I'd noticed the others were uncomfortable around him and did their best to steer clear. He worked—and practiced—alone. And the other operatives and soldiers breathed a collective sigh of relief over that preference.

In his early missions, certain soldiers chomped at the bit to work with him. They'd volunteered to assist him when rounding up donors and eliminating obstacles—namely parents, spouses, or anyone else who got in the way. His extreme methods were effective, but abhorrent enough that one mission was enough for them. Word quickly spread, and after A36's first two missions requests to accompany him came to a grinding halt. That suited him just fine.

After brutal storms the night before, the sun shone bright on this cloudless, fall morning. I inhaled the mossy smell of damp earth as the ground squished beneath my feet. The air was still. Not even a faint breeze blew through the canopied tree leaves of burnished orange, brown, and yellow.

Which is why I noticed movement in a large shrub ten yards to my right overlooking the range. A bigger movement than any creatures in this area would make. The bush was large enough to camouflage a human. I darted to the left and took cover behind the closest tree. Chancing a quick peek, I clocked two military boots, toes pointed downward, protruding from the base of the foliage.

I whipped back behind the tree. Why would someone be camouflaged in the shrub, lying on their stomach to watch A36? People had weird reasons for their actions, but my gut told me something was off here. More information was required. I crept several yards closer, maintaining cover as much as possible. The boots twitched slightly. The person was still alive, but from this angle there was no way I could identify whose feet were in them. I fanned left for a better look.

When I chanced a glance around the tree, I sucked in a breath. Colonel Ackerman lay on his stomach with a sniper rifle trained down into the bowl. A36 was the only person on the range. What the actual hell was this?

From all indications, Ackerman planned to assassinate A36. Asher.

I had only seconds before he took a shot. The damp earth absorbed the sound of my feet hitting the ground as I sprinted the short distance between us. At the last second, Ackerman turned in my direction, his eyes widening in shock. I dove and landed on his back, ripped the rifle from his hands, then rolled to the side and scrambled to my feet, the weapon pointed at him. He raised his hands slowly as he glowered at me. His reddened cheeks told me he was humiliated I'd gotten the jump on him.

"Ackerman, I may not be the smartest guy in the Colony, but from where I'm standing, this looks like an assassination attempt on Silas's prized possession."

His face darkened, and he squared his jaw in defiance. An explanation wouldn't be given freely, so I played the winning card. "I could take you down to the range and let you talk with A36. Explaining why you wanted to kill him would make his day. But probably not as much as punishing you for that crazy idea. You're damn lucky his ammo fire prevented him from hearing us, but if I were you, I'd keep my voice down. You know how sensitive his hearing is."

His eyes darted toward the range. Fear radiated off him like a cornered, wounded animal. It was clear A36 petrified Ackerman. I got that. Plenty of people felt the same. But why kill him? It's not like he and Ash or A36 had a history of altercations. He'd aided Dr. Everly in keeping Asher and Brynn here against their will, so if he wanted A36 dead, why not kill him then? He'd had the perfect opportunity the many times Everly had shocked Ash unconscious.

"Fine. I'll talk. That... *thing* deserves to die. Haven't you seen what he's done to people? He's a machine. No thoughts or feelings. No remorse. He tears people apart like he's ripping open a present."

I shrugged. Although it pained me, I had a role to play. "That's what they built him to do."

Ackerman shook his head, incredulous. "And you're okay with that? You condone his actions?"

"We all have our jobs to do. Mine is to relay orders from Silas to A36. How he chooses to carry out those orders isn't my responsibility. I make sure he completes his missions and then report back to Silas." And I was grateful every day I didn't have to see what became of A36's targets. I'd experienced enough carnage to last me a lifetime. "When did you decide it was your job to pass judgment on him? You forget I was there when you worked with Everly? Because of your soldiers, I nearly died. Who judges you? You think you're any better?"

He grimaced. "Everly was insane. All she cared about was making that boy into the killer he is now, then serving him on a silver platter to Silas. She deserved what he did to her. A36 is a monstrosity. Now Silas has plans to breed him like a dog and make his progeny just like him."

Silas's plan of an army of little A36s was a whole other shop of horrors I couldn't deal with right now. Ackerman was front and center and needed to be handled. An idea niggled at the back of my mind. It might be insane. It risked exposing me, and if things went the wrong way, I couldn't allow Ackerman to leave this range. But what if we could use him? If he'd turned against the Colony, he'd certainly be a valuable asset to the Insurgents. His connections reached far beyond these gates and could help rally allies. Could I trust him? I had to play this very carefully.

"What was your plan, Ackerman? If you'd killed him, which probably would have failed considering his advanced healing capacity—"

"He wouldn't have survived a headshot," he interrupted.

I shrugged. "Maybe. There's no confirmation on that. But what was your plan after he dropped? Just leave him out on the range to be found, then you go back to business as usual and hope Silas never found out? Being a military man, you can't expect me to believe you didn't have an end game."

His narrowed eyes evaluated me. Maybe he wondered if *he* could trust *me*. Did he suspect my own treason? If so, he'd never reported me to Silas. I was still breathing.

"I'm dead anyway." He sighed. "Coming clean can't hurt. I was going to leave. I've been a military man all my life. Followed every order I've been given, even when I disagreed with them. But this..." He gestured down the hill toward A36. "It's wrong. Sending this boy out to slaughter people just because Silas gives the order?" He huffed out a breath. "Most of the time, I'm not sure Silas even has a reason. He's consumed by power, and I don't want to be a part of his corrupt vision anymore. I figured I'd take out A36, slip through the gates, then find someplace off the grid to live a quiet life. No more violence."

This was huge. My gamble had paid off, and it looked like the odds had veered in my favor for a change. Ackerman turning could be the break we needed. He was planning to leave, and something like that didn't just happen overnight. Arrangements and contingencies had to be made. He'd disagreed with Silas for quite a while and was ready to cut and run. Killing A36 wasn't something he could just apologize for and then get back to work. His actions were permanent and irreconcilable. He could help us.

I slowly lowered the rifle. "You can put your hands down." Suspicion flashed in his eyes, but he did as I asked and stood. Once I let him in on everything we'd been doing, there was no going back. This was a game changer. Talk about your pivotal moments. I inhaled deeply, then let out my breath slowly.

"How would you like to do something positive with your life for a change?" He raised a brow in question. "Despite obvious appearances, I've been working against Silas and the Colony for months along with help from the Insurgents. I want to take him down as badly as you, and I think you could be as asset. Your military connections both here and in other territories could be a tremendous help to us."

He stared at me a long moment as he weighed his options. "What about him?" he asked, gesturing toward A36. "He's Silas's errand boy. Take him out, Silas loses power and reach."

"Nothing happens to A36. That's nonnegotiable."

"You saw what he did to my soldiers when you led them to the compound all those months ago. He slaughtered them like animals and never looked back. Have you seen what he does in the field?"

"He reacted that way because I pushed Ash to his breaking point. I was taking away the person he loves most in the world, and he needed A36 to get her back. Your soldiers stood in his path."

"He's a killing machine without a soul. He can't be allowed to live."

"I know exactly what he is. I also know *who* he is. Despite what he was built to be, the person inside is nothing like A36."

Ackerman huffed out a breath. "Not from where I'm sitting."

"You've only known him as Asher when he was fighting to save Brynn or as A36. Asher only turned over control because he couldn't bear to carry out the orders Silas gives him. He still believes if he disobeys, Silas will have his family killed. Asher is nothing like this. He'd rather die himself than let a hostage suffer another minute in harvest facilities."

Ackerman narrowed his eyes and crossed his arms over his chest. "What do you mean he still believes? Silas had trackers put on Anna and Brynn."

"To gain back the Insurgents' trust, I told Paige and Brynn about the trackers. I was there when Paige took out Brynn's and destroyed it. Silas knows he doesn't have tabs on them anymore but isn't concerned about it since A36 has fallen into line. Asher doesn't know. A36 has no family, and right now there's no way to let Asher know his is safe." I sighed heavily. "I vowed to return Asher to his family to help make up for what I've done. It's a drop in the bucket, but at least it's a start. You can help us or not. Your choice."

He jutted out his chin in defiance. "And if I say no?"

"Geez, Ackerman," I rolled my eyes. "I thought you were smart. Obviously, I'd have to kill you. I can't take the chance you'd go back to Silas. Too much is riding on this."

"What's your plan for A36?"

"There's only one. Brynn is our Hail Mary. I've got to get them together. If she can't bring Asher back, no one can."

"And if she fails?"

"Then you'll be down two Insurgents. No way A36 would let us live."

He considered me a moment longer, then shrugged. "I guess we're partners. I always liked Anna, and that Brynn's a spitfire. Should be an adventure working with her."

I offered my hand, and we shook on the deal. "Brynn's likely to bite your face off. I'd keep my distance if I were you. Now it's time for you to go back and play nice with Silas. I'll be in touch."

●   ●   ●   ●

It had been several days since I'd recruited Ackerman to our team, and Paige agreed everything he brought to the table gave us an edge. I wanted to allow myself a moment of hope, a small fiesta, even a fleeting one, but I was afraid I'd curse our good fortune. We still had so much work ahead of us. If I let myself breathe for a minute, we could lose any ground we'd gained. Celebrations would come later. A blow-out party that would last for days. Weeks even.

For now, I had to keep on blinders and stay focused.

I sat in my sparsely decorated office. Silas had encouraged me to make it my own, to let it reflect my personality, but I chose not to display any personal items. I preferred not to give the Colony any more pieces of myself than I had to. I sighed heavily and opened the file containing Silas's latest operative requests. Sending these tweeners out on assignments to commit various crimes and engage in nefarious activities hadn't been my dream job when I was younger. Sometimes you never knew where life would take you, but this was one job I prayed would end soon. My brow furrowed as I looked over the list. When Silas had first put me in this position, at any given time the percentage of our operatives in the field ranged from seventy-five percent to ninety percent. We'd even had a backlog of assignments since the kids also required some downtime. I'd noticed the number gradually dwindling in the past couple months, but hadn't given much thought to it. Actually, I'd been grateful to have even a small reprieve from putting these kids' lives in danger. I never knew if I'd see them again once they left my office on assignment.

The list from Silas this week was the shortest yet, and it puzzled me. Heavy repeat customer territories who sent weekly requests had all but vanished. It could make a person think maybe the world had finally decided to shun Silas's way of life and live peacefully, but I knew better than that. Some of the worst monsters in this world were humans themselves and the horrid things they did to each other.

There's no way Silas would let this go. He'd expect answers soon. I needed to be proactive and start digging around. Before I could begin, a message popped up from Ackerman marked urgent. Other than mutual meetings with Silas, we'd agreed to limit contact to a minimum. Basically, only if we needed to meet or in case of emergency. My heart rate sped up at the thought of what his urgent message might contain. I knew this could all be over at any minute, and my head could wind up on a stake, but I prayed this wasn't the end. We were close, I could feel it. I clicked on the message.

One of my contacts sent me these photos taken an hour ago. I've worked with him for years and trust him without question. What the actual hell is going on?

I opened the attached photos and dropped my data pad to the desk where it landed with a thud. This had to be a mistake. There's no way these were recent. Impossible. I picked up the pad again and clicked through the photos, my eyes wide in disbelief. Ice ran through my veins at the implications of what this could mean.

The heads of two territories, Flores from Grales and Kimathi from Baithe, who'd accepted Silas's offers of genetic stripping were eliminated on his orders so he could maintain power in their areas. According to these photos, they'd been alive and well just an hour ago. They'd met with several other leaders and military officers I recognized.

Ackerman was right. What the actual hell was going on here? I didn't need to check my files to see which operative had eliminated them because Silas had requested the same operative on both assignments. Someone he trusted implicitly.

Elsa.

15

DECLAN

I lounged casually in the overstuffed armchair in Elsa's quarters, feet propped on the glass coffee table and ankles crossed. Picking her lock would only have challenged a novice, so I'd gained access in less than thirty seconds. You'd think someone with her level of paranoia would have extra security measures. Maybe she's just too trusting of her neighbors and assumed no one would have the nerve to intrude into her private space. Guess this would be her first lesson in something she should have learned a long time ago.

Discovering her targets were still alive was mind-blowing. I'm talking stuck-my-wet-finger-into-an-electric-socket kind of shock. By all appearances, she was the perfect "daughter" to Silas. She did everything he asked, and her success rate in the field was nearly perfect. By all appearances. She'd denounced Asher as family and rebuffed any of his attempts at a reconciliation, which in my opinion was the final nail in his coffin. She'd brought on the rise of A36. If Silas was suspicious or had any concerns about Elsa, he hadn't relayed them to me.

By my calculations, it had taken her months of covert work and planning to get to this point. Maybe I was horribly wrong, but I assumed we shared the same goal—annihilating Silas and the Colony. If we pooled our efforts, our timeline for bringing down the Colony could make an enormous leap. This nightmare could be over in a matter of weeks instead of months. Elsa was a secretive, stubborn girl. Getting her to play nice with others, especially me, wouldn't come easy.

I glanced at the time. She'd returned from a mission just over an hour ago. History told me she'd wait until the last minute to contact me about debriefing. I'd broken in before she was due back, so I'd had time to nose around her apartment. Remembering her bedroom in Silas's quarters, I'd been prepared to shield my eyes from an assault of pink but was relieved to discover her personal choices leaned toward homey and comfy. Guess the pink explosion had truly been Silas's and Marilee's doing. I hadn't come across any evidence that indicated what she'd been up to. The girl was careful.

On the surface, her residence looked welcoming—cozy couches, lots of pillows, books on the shelves. But when you looked closer, really evaluated it with a discerning eye, it was all staged. Dishes that still appeared pristine, furniture with no wear and tear, books by popular authors that had never been opened. Nothing personal adorned the shelves or tables. Elsa lived here, but she didn't *live* here. The only personal item I'd found was a picture taped under her nightstand drawer. She, along with her parents, sister, and Asher, were gathered around a Christmas tree by a fireplace. That spoke volumes to me. How she'd even smuggled it in and kept it from Silas all these years was a mystery.

I picked up a book to leaf through, then sat back and recrossed my ankles on the coffee table. On the outside, my demeanor was relaxed and confident, even after breaking into a place where I was anything but welcome. On the inside, I was tightly coiled and ready to spring. Elsa was a trained killer, and I was someone she'd as happily decapitate as speak to me. I was invading the privacy of her home. This could turn ugly in the blink of an eye. An image of my brain matter and bone fragments splattered on her rug flashed through my mind, Elsa standing over it with a very satisfied, glorious grin on her face.

Between Brynn and Elsa, I'd had my fill of visions lately where they'd hurt or murdered me. If they ever joined forces, my days could be limited.

Footsteps approached the door and stopped. There was a pause before she keyed in her code. She already sensed something wasn't right. The door swung open and Elsa, her back to me, closed the door then shrugged off her bag. Instead of hanging it on the hook by the door, she spun and threw it at me. I ducked as it flew over my head and crashed into the bookcase behind me.

"What the hell are you doing here, Declan?" She faced me, gun drawn and pointed at my head.

"I came to ask you why your highest profile marks, Flores and Kimathi, are still alive." As her finger started to pull the trigger, I hurled the book I'd been holding toward her. Her eyes widened in surprise as the shot went wide, the gun knocked from her hand.

For one long moment, we scrutinized each other and our respective motives, then she snatched a knife from her boot and flung it at me. I dropped to the floor, but heard it whizz by my ear before embedding itself in the chair in the exact spot my heart had just been. She leaped over the coffee table and landed on my back.

In hindsight, I really should have been better prepared.

"Elsa," I grunted, "I'm not here to hurt you." She might be lethal and trained to kill, but I'd also had hand to hand combat training with the Insurgents. And had at least eighty pounds on her. With her still on my back, arms wrapped around my throat in a choke hold, my vision started to darken. Strength waning, I rose from the floor and flung myself backward onto the glass coffee table. It shattered and Elsa shrieked in pain, but the impact caused her hold on my neck to loosen. I took advantage of it and quickly stood and whirled around to face her. "Can we please talk about... aaaah!" I yelled as she plunged a large glass shard into my thigh.

She scrambled away from the table and dived behind the couch where her gun had landed moments earlier. Knowing she'd come up shooting and my life expectancy rate had taken a sudden, severe drop, I leaped behind the couch opposite hers and drew my own gun from my jacket. Which is how I really should have started this whole intervention. Odds were there would have been significantly less blood loss. On my part, at least.

Using the sofa as a shield, I poked my head up, gun pointed only to find Elsa mirroring my stance. Blood trailed down the side of her face from a cut on her forehead. Her eyes were cold and emotionless, weapon steady and aimed at my head. Stalemate.

"I don't care if you're Silas's shadow, Declan. I'll kill you right now and face his consequences. You have no right to be here. Now what do you want?"

My chest heaved from exertion. Seriously? She wasn't even breathing hard? "I'm here because I think we can help each other. I suspect you've formed alliances with other territories while going against Silas's orders. I've been working with the Insurgents and Ackerman to bring him down."

A crease formed between her brows as she considered my words. "Why should I believe you? Maybe you're just saying that to convince me to cooperate with you. Maybe Silas found out what I've done and when I drop my gun, you'll kill me."

So, she maintained a healthy distrust of Colony folks after all. Or it could have just been because it was me. "All right, Elsa, one of us has to take a chance and trust the other, and if it's not soon, I'm going to pass out from loss of blood." I dropped my gun onto the sofa, raised my hands, then stood. She slowly rose, but kept her weapon poised on me in case of any sudden moves. "Losing blood here."

She lowered her gun and shoved it back into her jacket. "Fine. You don't have to be so dramatic about it, Princess."

I totally resented that remark. "Towel? Please?"

She pointed a finger at me. "Don't bleed on my carpet." While she left the room to get a towel—at least I really hoped that's where she was going—I limped over to the kitchen table and dropped into a chair. Since it sat on tile, her precious rug would be preserved. Forget that I was bleeding to death. She came back into the room, taking her sweet time I might add, carrying a towel and first aid kit.

"If this is the way you welcome people into your home, it's no wonder you don't have any friends. Just saying."

"I didn't welcome you into my home, Declan. This is how I greet unwanted visitors." I grimaced as she yanked the glass shard from my leg. "Take off your pants."

I cocked an eyebrow. "Now that's a much better welcome."

She rolled her eyes. "Don't flatter yourself. I need to bandage your leg. Trust me, a medical emergency is the only reason I'd ask you to shed clothing."

After she'd stopped the bleeding, added a few stitches, and bandaged my wound, I pulled my pants back on. Her loss. Elsa got two bottles of water from the fridge and tossed one to me, more like at me, then slid into the chair at the opposite end of the table.

I was more interested in pressing the cold bottle to my wound, but I drank from it instead. "Tell me why your targets are still alive."

"First tell me how you found out."

"Ackerman. He has military contacts everywhere and someone sent him photos of the two of them meeting."

She muttered something under her breath about stupid leaders ignoring safety precautions. "Fine. The deal with Flores didn't sit well with me. He had a wife and young children, and I didn't want them to wind up like my own family, so I hid them. I faked proof of their deaths to Silas. When he gave me the assignment to take out Kamathi, I knew I could make an ally out of him, too. They were surprisingly cooperative when I explained what Silas had in store for them."

Impressive. I'd never suspected a thing. "You've got both of them in your pocket? A plan in place?"

She took a drink of water then set down the bottle. "That's why they were meeting. Planning strategy. Gathering more allies. Silas has made an impressive number of enemies, and plenty were willing to jump on board."

"You surprised me, Elsa. These days, it's rare anyone does. I thought you were all in with Silas, a Colony supporter through and through. Someone who'd go down with the ship when this was all over."

The corner of her mouth turned up into a half smile. "For the longest time, I blamed Asher for everything that happened to us. If he hadn't left Cami and me alone, my family would still be alive. I truly believed that. Once I got older and gained some insight, I thought about that day a lot. Bits and fragments of memories would come to me at the strangest times, and I began to piece them together. I've known for a while what Silas was doing was wrong. I haven't forgotten everything my parents taught us." She studied her water bottle intently and peeled away part of the label. "I just lost my way for a while. And that's something I'll have to live with."

This girl just continued to surprise me. So much had happened to her. She'd experienced so many tragedies in her life already and endured all of it alone. That hard core exterior of hers hid a gooey interior. Someone who struggled with her past just as much as I did with my own.

I slowly reached my hand across the table and placed it on her forearm. She flinched when I touched her but didn't jerk away. "We all lose our way sometimes, Elsa. Don't forget who you're talking to. All we can do now is try to rectify the wrongs any way we can."

She nodded but kept her gaze on the bottle she gripped with both hands. "That's what I'm trying to do. It's all I can do. I just need to keep Silas in the dark until everything is in place." Her gaze met mine. "We could really do this, Declan. If we can bring everyone together the numbers would far outweigh Silas's army."

More allies. A bubble of happiness surged inside me. With the Insurgents, Ackerman and his contacts, and now Elsa's territories, there just might be a light at the end of the tunnel after all.

She looked up sideways at me and lifted a brow. "Ackerman? Seriously? Thought he was loyal to the bone."

"I caught him trying to snipe A36 because Ackerman believes him to be a monstrous killing machine. Discussions commenced, truths revealed, and now he's on our side." I cracked my water bottle open and took another long swallow.

She huffed out a breath. "I'd try that myself if I thought I could get away with it. Or if it was even possible. He's Silas's pet. He'll do anything he's told."

I wiped my mouth on my sleeve. "Don't be so sure. Until a few hours ago, I thought you were Silas's pet. Your brother is still in there, Elsa. We'll bring Asher back. Do you really believe those things you said to him before A36 stepped in? Those were some seriously heartless words."

She scratched at a patch of dried blood on her hand. It could have been mine just as easily as hers. "I didn't know if he was Asher or A36. There was no way to know where his loyalties lay at that point. If I'd taken him into my confidence and said the wrong thing, he'd have informed Silas, and all my work would have been for nothing."

"He would have helped you, but he'd never have been able to carry out Silas's orders as Asher. It would have destroyed him. What you said about him not being your family pushed him to the edge. He had no choice but to turn to A36. As far as he knows, it saved the people he loves."

Elsa narrowed her eyes. "What do you mean as far as he knows? I thought Silas had trackers placed on them."

I shook my head. "He did, but I played that card to gain Paige's and Brynn's trust and helped destroy the trackers. Silas doesn't know where they are, but he has no reason to tell A36 that. Family doesn't matter to him anyway. Asher is buried so deep, I doubt he'd hear even if someone told him the trackers were gone."

She frowned. "You trust him?"

"A36? Never. We need Asher."

"You can't just flip a switch and bring him back. What's your plan for luring him out?"

"Brynn. She's probably the only one who can reach him. I'm supposed to get her in a room with him."

"Well, you can't sneak her in through these gates, so what's your plan for getting them together?"

An idea popped into my head. It would be tricky. Putting anything past A36 was next to impossible, but if I had another assassin involved? "I think you might be the answer to that question."

After hours of talking, comparing notes, planning, and sharing information, I left Elsa's apartment feeling lighter than I had in weeks. She had some powerful allies in her pocket. Paige would be ecstatic, in her own understated way, of course. Timelines needed to be moved up.

But the most important thing right now was to get Asher back. If Brynn couldn't reach him, none of this would work. This could end with A36 slaughtering all of us.

16

BRYNN

I wiped my sweaty palms on my pants and resumed wearing down the already threadbare rug with my pacing. The thought of seeing Asher in the next few minutes had my heart racing, but I reminded myself again he was A36 and not the boy I'd loved for more than half my life. Willingly putting myself in a room with a cold-blooded assassin who'd just as soon kill me for wasting his time than talk to me was taking a monumental risk. But with all my heart, I trusted that Asher could regain control like he had the night we'd tried to raid the harvest facility. That he possessed the strength to overcome A36 for that one brief glimpse was what I desperately clung to.

Declan had arranged the meeting in a safehouse owned by the Colony. Convincing A36 he was acting on Silas's orders was the only way to get him here. Knowing he was likely to believe a story about meeting another assassin, Declan had thought about using Elsa to lure A36 here, but then decided against it. He didn't want to risk the life of another person. Especially one who remained unconvinced Asher was worth saving. I planned on having words with Elsa when this was all over.

It had stunned me to learn Elsa had been busy engineering her own war against Silas. She'd made some mighty gutsy moves. Getting the heads of two other territories on our side tipped the scales even further in our favor, but like Declan, I wasn't celebrating yet. Too many things could go sideways. More people could be killed. People I cared about. According to Declan, my reassurance that Asher could leash A36 again was the only thing that prevented Elsa from executing him. From his description, she had no qualms about using A36's trust in her to take him by surprise. Not exactly trust—he didn't trust anyone—he tolerated her presence and believed their goals were aligned. It was hard to reconcile the clumsy little girl who'd trailed after Asher and Noah with the calculating assassin she'd become. Family or not, if she made a move against Asher, she'd have to get through me first.

The heavy growl of an engine and the crunch of tires on gravel told me Declan and A36 had arrived. Two car doors slammed. I closed my eyes, inhaled deeply, and breathed out slowly. Voices drifted in through the cracked window.

I moved closer and chanced a peek of A36 through the thin curtains. Every movement was precise. His gaze darted over the house and the area around it, a predator evaluating his surroundings. "Explain why we're here. This is outside mission parameters." It was Asher—and it wasn't. A36 didn't waste words. He spoke in clipped sentences, and his words were sharp enough to slash through muscle and bone.

"I told you, it's a new contact who reached out. Since Elsa was held up, she said you were the only person she trusted to come in her place." To Declan's credit, there wasn't a hint of a waver in his voice with the lies he told. A36 would have immediately picked up on it and suspected a deception.

"You're perspiring. Your heart rate is escalated."

"It's hot outside, and I'm sweating, all right? And maybe I missed some workouts. Relax, A36. Not everyone's a genetically enhanced superhuman."

I waited in the kitchen until they entered the house and closed the door behind them. I wasn't sure how A36 would react if I was the first thing he saw. Getting him inside and easing him into the situation seemed to be the safest option. Not that there was anything safe about this whole scenario.

"Where is she?" Maybe it wasn't exactly Ash's voice, but I still recognized the hints of annoyance and impatience. That much hadn't changed. He'd used the same tone with me when I refused to take safer positions while we planned rescue missions at the compound.

He wouldn't wait patiently for long. It was go time. I turned the corner and stepped into the room. A36's eyes flashed in recognition then narrowed in suspicion. His fingers twitched and his muscles tightened. He didn't trust me or this situation. Although he and Declan carried weapons, I was unarmed by choice. Declan had loudly and repeatedly protested my decision, but the less I antagonized A36 the better. He needed to believe he still held all the power.

For now.

He quickly conducted a visual scan and noted the lack of a weapon on my person. He immediately scrutinized the room, calculated hiding places, then locked on the location where I'd stashed a gun. It was the only way Declan would agree to this meeting. If the situation went south, maybe one of us could get to it in time. The corner of A36's mouth twitched as his gaze found mine again.

He studied me, unmoving, unblinking. "You're an Insurgent, not a potential informant. Why are you here?" His voice was flat, devoid of any emotion. Again, he ignored Silas's orders of killing Insurgents on sight. It was encouraging.

Declan was on edge, and his hand inched toward the gun at his hip.

I shook my head slightly.

"I'll put you down before you reach it, Declan. You're a traitor, and I'll deal with you later." A36's gaze had never left mine. He'd only sensed Declan's movement.

I kept my hands to my side in an unthreatening manner and spoke calmly and evenly. "I'm not armed, and you're right. I'm not here to give information to the Colony."

"Then you're worthless to me. An enemy to be eliminated."

"No," I said gently. "I'm not your enemy. I want to help *you*, not the Colony."

His expression was wary but curious. A36 tilted his head. His brow furrowed as if I were a puzzle to solve. "Help me? The only thing of value you could offer me is the locations of Insurgent compounds."

"I want to offer you something far more valuable. Memories. Family. A life."

A hint of uncertainty flashed in his eyes, but he schooled his features back into an unfeeling appearance. "You're wasting my time. I have a mission to get back to."

"If I'm preventing you from accomplishing your mission, and you've already classified me as an enemy, then why haven't you eliminated me?" My words taunted him, but I had to trust that A36 would respect and maybe even enjoy a direct challenge. The lack of any threatening moves on his part so far was promising.

He folded his arms over his chest and looked down at me. There might have been a hint of admiration in his gaze. "A good question. Why have I allowed you to live?"

"Because you'd never hurt me."

He barked out a stilted, hollow laugh. It was nothing like Asher's weird cackling laugh that never failed to put a smile on my face. Even when I was furious with him over something.

"Do you have a death wish? If so, I can grant that in seconds."

I shook my head. "You're incapable of killing me, even if I begged you to. Deep down you know that."

He stood taller, raised his chin defiantly and looked down his nose at me. "I'm tired of this game. Let's finish it." He advanced toward me, but I held my ground. His hand reached for my throat. I didn't even flinch. In my peripheral vision, I caught Declan's movement as he rushed forward.

"Brynn!" With my hands still at my side, I motioned for him to stay where he was. We'd talked about this, and I'd instructed him that no matter what happened, he wasn't to make a move on A36. I'd handle him on my own. We both knew that if this failed, if I couldn't raise Asher, Declan and I were dead and any hope of destroying the Colony would die with us. A36 would take our bodies back to Silas and then make a hit list. He'd track down anyone who had a hand in this betrayal. Declan taking this leap of faith with me spoke volumes.

As his fingers grazed my throat, I said one word. "Asher." His face froze in horror. He retreated abruptly, and something like fear flashed in his eyes, but then disappeared just as quickly. "I'm not Asher. Not anymore." His voice was gritty and strained.

I moved cautiously toward him. He staggered backward until his back was against the wall. "Yes, you are. Asher is still in there. He chooses to let you be in control, allows you to use his body."

"No!" he growled. "*I'm* in control. He's been gone for months, and he's never coming back." His features twisted in anger, A36 charged toward me.

His massive hands shot out and gripped both my upper arms. Still, I didn't fight him.

"Asher, I'm here. It's Brynn," I said.

"Stop! Quit saying his name!" He punctuated his words by shaking me, and my head rocked backwards.

"Let Ash speak."

His hands still gripped my arms. His muscles trembled as he fought to maintain control. I had no doubt A36 wanted to kill me, but at his core was my Ash, and I had faith in him.

"I know your heart," I whispered.

Those words, the same words I'd repeated whenever he doubted himself, when he questioned what he was after discovering how he'd come into this world and the reason he'd been created, had an immediate effect on him. Even as his grip tightened, his eyes rolled back in his head. His whole body shook.

"What's happening?" Declan took a step in my direction.

"Stay back. Asher's fighting."

I winced at how tightly he held me, then his arms dropped as he staggered away from me and stumbled into a table. The lamp setting atop it tumbled to the ground and shattered. His eyes found mine, and my heart clenched at his wounded animal look. I moved toward him, but he held up a quivering hand.

"Don't... Stay... away," he said through clenched teeth.

"Asher..."

A36's body crashed into the wall behind him. "No!" he roared. Perspiration covered his face as he fought against Asher and slumped to the floor. Every limb trembled violently.

"Should we try to restrain him?" Declan asked. "If he keeps going like this, he'll hurt himself. Or maybe that's what he's trying to do."

"Brynn..." His voice was muffled with his head hung between his knees, but I'd know it anywhere after spending most of my life with him. It was Asher. His head slammed backward. Cracks spider-webbed the plastered wall.

I sank to my knees in front of him and pleaded with him. "Fight, Ash. You can do this. We need you. *I* need you." The violent trembling stopped. Asher's body stilled, then went limp as he fell over onto his side. He didn't move.

He wasn't moving.

Every other sound in the room vanished, like I was in a vacuum. All strength left my limbs, and I nearly toppled onto Asher's lifeless body. I looked down at my chest, sure I'd see a hemorrhaging, gaping hole. Only a fatal wound could hurt this much. This must be how he'd felt when he thought I'd died.

No. I refused to believe our story would end this way.

Someone grabbed my shoulder. It was Declan. He sank to the floor beside me. Sound came back to me in a sudden roar. "Is he... " He couldn't finish the sentence.

My hand felt disconnected from my body as I inched it toward Asher's neck and felt for a beat. Prayed for a pulse. My life would end with his if I found none. But there it was. Beneath my fingers was a faint throbbing, getting stronger with every pump of his heart. Sweet relief rushed through me, and I sagged against Declan for support.

"He's alive," I said, my voice quivering. I gently leaned forward and brushed his cheek with my fingertips. "Can you hear me?"

Asher's lids fluttered open, and his searching gaze was unfocused. Then his eyes found mine. "Brynn?" He pushed himself into a sitting position and raised a hand to cup my face. "Are you really here?" A wave of fear rolled over his face. "Anna and Noah, are they alright?"

I nodded, tears streaming down my face. "They're safe." Over the months we'd been apart, I'd put up a good front telling everyone we'd bring Asher home. Behind a door deep inside me I tried to keep locked, I questioned whether it was really possible. Sometimes, especially late at night when I couldn't sleep, that door cracked open, doubt slithered out and ran rampant through my mind before I wrangled it back inside and locked it up even tighter. If I ever saw him again, I wasn't sure who—or what—he'd be.

His thumbs brushed away my tears, and then he pulled me against his chest. His arms encircled me, and his lips found mine. It wasn't gentle. Months of barely restrained fear, anguish, and anger, and my consuming love for him rushed forward, ecstatic to finally have an outlet. Seconds, minutes—maybe days passed, I really didn't care. Asher was finally here.

And then someone cleared their throat. Declan. I'd forgotten he was still in the room.

"Um, sorry to interrupt, guys, but we've got a lot to talk about."

Asher broke off the kiss, and his head whipped in Declan's direction. Declan had moved across the room to give us what little privacy he could. I guess he could have gone outside, but then we might have gotten a little carried away. Better that he stayed.

Asher's expression was murderous. "What the hell is he doing here?" Even as I answered him, he gently pushed me to the side and slid toward Declan.

"It's fine. He's with us."

"No, he's not. You were always right not to trust him. He's Silas's right-hand man. He threatened you, Noah, and Anna," Asher said, pushing against the wall to stand.

Declan raised his hands in surrender. "I'm working with the Insurgents, I swear. I helped the three of them escape, and I tried to help you, too."

Ash narrowed his eyes and flexed his hands. "If that's true, then you'd be dead. Silas would have had you killed."

I rose quickly and moved between them before this escalated and placed my hands against Asher's chest. "I didn't want to believe it either, but it's true. Silas is convinced he's loyal to the Colony, but Declan's been feeding us intel and working from the inside for months. He brought you here, to me."

Ash continued to glare at Declan, turning this information over in his mind. I knew he believed me, but his memory was undoubtedly riddled with holes and blank spots. Syncing Oz who'd given up the location of our compound with the Declan that stood before him was a struggle. It was weeks before I'd felt even an inkling of trust in him. After what he'd done for me today, I'd be indebted to him for the rest of my life—something I never dreamed I'd say about Declan.

"I swear it's true, Ash. I've been your handler for months now. Elsa's, too. Do you remember anything?"

His brow furrowed, and I felt his body back down a notch. He didn't remember. I prayed he didn't recall anything he'd done as A36. Taking his hand, I led him over to the sofa. Declan eased into the chair facing us and gnawed on his thumbnail.

Ash slumped back against the cushion, dropped his gaze to the floor, and shook his head. "The last thing I remember is tearing my room apart after Silas told me the vile things he wanted me to do. I refused, but he gave me no choice. You were there, Declan."

"I'm sorry for what I said, Ash. You know I'd never hurt Anna, Brynn, or Noah. I had to maintain my cover, keep up the illusion of a dutiful servant to Silas."

Ash nodded as if accepting his apology. "I also remember fighting with Elsa. She rejected me, said we weren't family." I squeezed his hand, knowing the pain her words caused him. Family meant everything to Ash, and he'd never gotten over losing his sisters. I knew Elsa wasn't the sweet, clumsy girl from our childhood, but when Declan said she was alive, I'd hoped she and Ash could rely on each other. Look how that turned out.

"Silas had me in a vise grip. I saw no way to leave and still keep everyone I loved safe. Was that only a few days after you left?" He raised his head and met my gaze. "My mind is really fuzzy."

"No," I answered softly. "I left the Colony almost seven months ago."

"Seven months? I've lost seven months of my life?" His expression contorted in agony, and my heart twisted for him and what he was about to learn. I'd gladly shoulder some of his pain, make it my own if it was possible.

"A36 took over for you," Declan said.

Asher's shoulders drooped, and he squeezed his eyes shut. "That last night when I tore up my room. I knew I couldn't do what Silas wanted, but A36 could." A single tear slid from the corner of his eye, and his voice hitched. "How bad was it, Declan? How many people did I kill?"

Declan looked at me with a panicked expression. We'd expected this question from Asher, knew there was no getting around it. He'd want to know the devastation and damage he'd caused. Giving him that answer might break him. Maybe enough that he'd retreat back into himself, and A36 would dominate again. It was too heavy a burden for him to bear right now. We'd deal with it later when we had time to sort it all out, and Asher had the support he needed. He'd need all of us.

"Asher, look at me." He tilted his head up, and his face was full of sorrow for all that he'd done. And all that he didn't yet know. "Whatever you did, it wasn't you. It was him. I promise you, we'll work through all of that later. Right now, our priority is to take out Silas and the Colony."

"We don't have much time," Declan added. "This detour extended the mission, and we can't let Silas or anyone else suspect something's going on. We've got a limited window before I need to get you back."

"Back?" Asher asked in disbelief. "What are you even saying? There's no way in hell that's happening. This is my chance to go back home to my family and the Insurgents."

This was another scenario we'd expected. Ash wanted to come home. I wanted him with me more than anything, but dismantling the Colony was bigger than us, and it had to take precedent. We'd never have a real life, and no one would ever be safe while Silas was still in power.

Asher put his arms around me and hugged me to his chest. My head fit perfectly underneath his chin just like it always had. I wanted to snuggle into him and stay right here, not think about everything we had ahead of us. He whispered, "I'm not leaving you again."

I waited a long moment before I pulled back, savoring that sliver of peace. "And I don't want you to, but we've spent months planning. For all this to work, you need to let Silas think you're still A36."

Declan leaned forward in his chair. "We have help, Ash. It's not just the Insurgents against Silas anymore. Anna has contacts within the Colony. We've also got some other irons in the fire that I'll tell you about later."

I knew he was referring to Elsa, but telling Ash about the danger she'd put herself in might not be the best idea right now. No matter what she'd said to him, Ash still thought of himself as her big brother, and his protective instincts were off the chart. We couldn't have him storming back to the Colony and blowing up everything Elsa had worked so hard to accomplish. I suspected Declan would tell Ash about Ackerman in due time. That reveal would come as an enormous surprise to him. "Silas seems unaware that we've been accumulating powerful allies. Pretty soon, life won't be all unicorns and rainbows for him. But for now, keeping in his good graces is my job. We need to pretend like today never happened, that A36 is still in control."

Asher stared wide-eyed at Declan. His interest was piqued, and I knew no matter his own needs, he'd put the welfare of others first and fight against Silas. "You've really been busy."

A grin split Declan's face, and his face flushed a light shade of red. "Yeah, well I've got a long list of things to make up for. But it's hopeful, you know? Like we're not alone in our fight anymore. There might even be a happily ever after for us out there."

"A lot of this hinges on you, Ash." I squeezed his hand. "Declan has been invaluable on the inside."

Asher smirked and raised an eyebrow in surprise. All he remembered was my predominantly adversarial relationship with Oz/Declan.

"Having you working alongside him, being that close to Silas, is an even bigger advantage."

"Can you do this?" Declan asked. "You can't let Silas get even a whiff that you're not A36."

Asher stared evenly at Declan. I knew him well enough to understand what was passing through his mind. Would he have to kill innocents? Force people into harvest facilities? Could he pretend to be A36 without causing suspicion?

"I don't really have a choice, do I? You have to brief me on everything going on while we travel back to the Colony. We're not talking gaps in time, Declan. Most of the last seven months are a blank canvas for me."

Declan's eyes darted to mine. Maybe Ash's memory would come back in short bursts, all at once, or never. For his sanity, I hoped for the latter. "I'll tell you what you need to know for now. Something else we need to discuss is your upcoming assignments."

Asher's face hardened, and he squared his jaw. I already knew the answer to that question. "I'll never kill for him again."

"How can you avoid it without making him suspicious?" Declan asked. "There's no way you can keep up this scenario as A36 if you defy his orders."

It was crucial that everyone believed Ash was still buried. If he slipped up, if there was even a hint he wasn't Silas's cold-blooded assassin, all our carefully crafted plans would come crashing down around us. There had to be some way to keep him out of the field.

"What if you were injured?" I asked.

Asher shook his head. "That won't work. I heal too quickly."

"There's nothing we can do that would put you out permanently, but what about for three to five days? Even a few days gives us enough time to get things rolling."

Asher rubbed his stubbled chin. "You know, that could work. After a break my bones heal in a few days, but if it was a bad break, we'd have extra time to prepare." He was silent as he considered it, then turned to Declan. "Run over my arm with the Jeep. It may take more than a few tries."

Declan balked at Ash's request. "Run over your arm? On purpose? What happens if you flake out and we have to fight our way out of the Colony?"

Ash snorted. "You can't tell me you wouldn't take some sort of perverse pleasure in running me over. And not to sound arrogant—"

"You? Never," Declan interrupted.

Ash raised a brow and continued. "But me fighting with one arm is worth about ten other operatives fighting with both."

Declan sighed loudly and shrugged. "All right. Let's get you splayed out in the driveway and commence with the breakage."

17

DECLAN

Silas knew.

He'd summoned me to his office. Told me to drop everything immediately, it was of utmost importance. Commanding my presence was nothing new, but the tone of his voice was different this time. Anxious. Tense. Enraged even. My gut churned at the fear I'd finally been discovered. It was business as usual around here as far as I knew, but this was outside the usual parameters. Red flags billowed high. Alarm bells shrieked.

After Asher and I had returned, Silas had been disappointed A36's injury benched him temporarily but didn't seem suspicious. He'd been too pleased with the progress A36 had made. I'd kept Asher hidden away as much as possible. When public appearances were unavoidable, I told him to wear his best serial killer face and growl at people who got too close, and he'd be just fine. People tended to keep their distance from A36 anyway.

We were so close, in the home stretch. The attack was scheduled in five days. Coordinating an operation of this magnitude seemed almost insurmountable, especially when so many of the players were in different locations and couldn't readily communicate with each other. Paige had handled it like the pro that she was. But all that careful planning could come crashing down in the next half hour.

I shoved my trembling hands into the pockets of my jacket and pasted my usual overly confident, am-I-not-the-sexiest-guy-you've-ever-seen look on my face.

The elevator doors opened, and Jade looked up from her desk. The flat tone of her voice and condescension in her eyes condemned me. "He's waiting. You're late."

"He contacted me less than five minutes ago."

"And every second after that you're late." She pointed toward Silas's door, her mouth set in a grim line. I wondered if she knew why he'd summoned me. Jade was too intelligent to be Silas's long-term assistant and not have her finger on the pulse of what went on around here.

I nodded at the guards on either side of his door, then swallowed hard, lifted my chin, and entered Silas's office. He stood with his back to me, hands clasped behind him as he gazed out over the city.

"Take a seat, Declan," he said, not turning around. Anger had seethed from him earlier, but he'd reined in his emotions. His voice was now cold and emotionless. Not that Silas was ever the warm and fuzzy type, but it was clear something wasn't right in his warped utopian world.

I crossed the marble floor to the black leather chair and eased down, not taking my eyes off him. Could he hear the hammering of my heart? I'd swear the high-ceilinged room amplified the thumping as it beat in my ears. I tried to slow my breath, but it was nearly impossible when every fiber of my being told me I'd walked smack into a precarious situation. My muscles were tensed and ready for flight. Fighting wasn't an option. Not alone. Too many people depended on me.

"How many agents do we currently have on assignment?"

I didn't need to check my data. The information was memorized. Silas demanded quick answers, and I always had them. "Three returned today, and ten agents are still out."

"And that's down twenty-five percent compared to previous months."

It wasn't a question. He was leading me somewhere. "Yes, sir. The numbers have steadily declined."

He slowly turned to face me, then placed his hands on the back of his desk chair and gripped it, his knuckles whitening. His piercing black eyes were like a laser probing my mind, and I felt the overwhelming need to protect my thoughts.

"After more than a decade of using our young operatives, the leaders of the two territories we recently made genetic harvesting agreements with, Adria and Taron, have broken off all ties. Genetic makeover requests are down significantly in Flores's territory of Grales and Kimathi's area of Baithen. The requests were high right before their deaths. A36 had his hands full with recruiting donors, but now I'm hearing reports of unrest among their citizens. To say I'm disappointed is putting it mildly."

"Of course," I nodded. "I've been puzzled myself. Our agents' positive outcomes in those territories are nearly perfect. A36 also reported the decreased demand for donors when he returned from his last assignment." I knew exactly why ties had been severed and demand had decreased. Elsa. She might be young, but the girl was a force of nature and apparently possessed superhuman persuasive powers.

"Excluding the positive outcomes, what other reason could they have for severing ties? Our agents provide a valuable service. Those territories are also aware of how successful our genetic harvesting program is and were eager to begin their own."

Sweat trickled down my back, but my voice remained steady. "I'm afraid I don't have an answer, sir. It's possible it has nothing to do with the agents. Is there some scenario I'm unaware of? Something happening within their territories that doesn't require our agents' skill sets? Perhaps they've heard about the decreased donor demand in the other territories and question instituting the program in their own areas."

His eyes narrowed as he considered my answer, and I fought the urge to look down at the floor and break his intense gaze. If I did, Silas would interpret it as a sign of guilt or dishonesty. After weighing my response a moment longer, he strode to the front of his desk, leaned against it and faced me, placing his hands on either side of his body. "I knew Adria's leader wavered on whether they should implement harvesting, so I let it go. I assumed she'd grown a conscience. When Preston from Taron territory ceased contact, I knew there was a problem. He spurned my attempts at communication, but his second in command, Logan, was a strong proponent of harvesting at our meetings. She contacted me and relayed some very disturbing confessions."

My pounding heart stuttered. This could be bad. Very bad. Elsa had paid a visit to Taron, but she'd assured me precautions had been taken, and they'd remain radio silent. After telling Preston about Silas's plans to take over territories after their leaders mysteriously died—coincidentally just months after beginning genetic harvesting—he'd immediately agreed to cease contact with Silas and ally with us. Logan had a history of been overly ambitious, but Preston seemed to have a handle on her and assured Elsa she would fall in line. Knowing Silas, I'm sure he made some kind of deal with Logan in exchange for information. He had a knack for sniffing out the weak links.

I leaned forward in my seat. I didn't have to feign interest in what might spew forth from Silas's mouth next. It could mean life or death for Elsa. And possibly Asher and me. "Did she have an explanation for why Taron had backed out?"

Silas pursed his lips. "Unfortunately, yes." His hands gripped the edge of the desk so hard I thought his knuckles might burst through his skin. "We've been betrayed. Someone has been meeting with the heads of territories and turning them against us."

Fear clawed at my throat, and I willed my body to fight the instinct to run. "Do you know who?"

"Without a doubt." Something like grief flashed across his face, but quickly disappeared. "It's Elsa."

The edges of my peripheral vision darkened, and a heavy ball of fear coiled in my stomach. He knew. Silas knew Elsa had betrayed him. Did he know we were working together? I shoved my panic to the side and focused. I still needed to play the game and keep us alive as long as I could. My eyes widened. "Elsa? But she's like your daughter and one of our most successful operatives. Are you certain, sir? Her identity has been confirmed?" He'd only mentioned the territories that had backed out. Maybe he didn't know she'd spared the lives of Flores and Kimathi after Silas sent her to eliminate them.

"Of course I've confirmed her identity. Now I know where her loyalties truly lie, what she really is." He slapped the edge of the desk he'd been gripping, and his voice rose. "She played me all these years! I took her in, and after all I've done for her, she's working to dismantle everything I've built." He narrowed his eyes and raised his chin in suspicion. "Were you aware of her deceit, Declan? Did she give you any reason to doubt her loyalty?"

My posture stiffened as I feigned surprise. "Absolutely not. From all appearances, Elsa was a consummate operative."

Silas nodded slowly as he considered my answer. "Since you debrief the operatives, the thought crossed my mind that you might be involved, maybe aided Elsa in some way. But I'm aware of what you've done for the Colony. You've been nothing but a devoted and trustworthy assistant."

"Thank you, sir." Dread threatened to steal my voice, but I had to ask the question. "Uh, how do you want to handle this?"

He ran a hand over his face, then gave me a pained stare. "I've been over every scenario and weighed the outcomes of each of them. Allowing her to live would be a sign of weakness no matter who she is. I have no choice but to eliminate her. Have A36 handle it."

"But she's his sister. Wouldn't you rather have someone else do it?"

"A36 is efficient, and he doesn't recognize familial relationships. Elsa has turned against us, Declan. Getting rid of her is your only priority right now, and I wanted it handled immediately. I expect confirmation of her death in an hour."

"Yes, sir. I'll let you know when it's done."

I rose from the chair on unsteady legs and doubted my ability to walk out of here and make it to the elevator. But I refused to fail Ash and Elsa now. Everything hinged on what I did in the next few minutes. Closing the door gently behind me, I walked stiffly past Jade's desk without acknowledging her for the first time since the day I'd first sauntered into Silas's office. My trembling hand pressed the button to summon the elevator.

"Declan, are you all right?" Jade asked.

I turned toward her and attempted a smile, but my face felt numb. The muscles weren't cooperating. "I'm fine. Everything's fine."

The doors slid open, and I stumbled inside. I'd been ordered to have Elsa killed. Silas expected confirmation within the hour. There was no way out of this, nothing I could say or do to smooth this over. Opening my data pad, I typed in our previously agreed on abort code and sent it to Elsa and Ash. There were four codes—individual ones in the event one of our covers was blown and a fourth meaning all three of us got out. That's the code I sent. If any of us called it, we dropped everything immediately and ran like hell. Only Elsa had been exposed, but when I didn't confirm her death within the hour, Silas would know I was an accomplice. Asher would also be gone, and it wouldn't take Silas long to connect the dots between the three of us.

Once we had Asher back, he, Elsa and I created an escape plan in the event the proverbial fecal matter hit the fan. We'd designated a place to meet in the hopes we could exit the Colony before anyone noticed our absence. Odds weren't in our favor—we knew this.

I contacted someone else who could help. The only person who might be able to give us an edge. Since it was traceable, I'd promised to never call from this comm pad unless it was an emergency. At this point my cover would be blown within the hour, so what the hell. We needed help.

"Declan?"

"Paige, Silas knows about Elsa. He gave me the order to have A36 kill her. We're coming in, and we need all the help we can get. If you've got any ideas, now's the time to share them."

She was silent a moment, but I'd swear I could feel her strategizing. "Go to your egress point. Aries 7 will meet you and offer assistance. Be safe." Paige terminated the connection.

Aries 7 was a long-time informant on the Colony for the Insurgents. Any information from that source had always been highly accurate. The only exception was when I'd died as Oz, but that had been a closely guarded secret. Even Silas hadn't known about me initially. Everly made the deal with me on her own in hopes of bringing in A36 and getting on Silas's good side again. For security reasons, only the Controller knew the identities of Insurgent informants. Only Paige and Noah were privy to the identity of Aries 7.

And I hadn't asked Paige who it was.

The elevator doors opened, and I hurried in the direction of the supply closet where I'd hidden a go-bag stuffed with cash and weapons. Knowing if and when it came time to haul ass I might not be able to get in my quarters, I'd stashed it somewhere more accessible.

I strode down the hallway as fast as I could without drawing suspicion, nodding to soldiers passing in the opposite direction. My heart pounded so fast and loud I wondered if they could hear it. Perspiration trickled down the back of my neck. The supply closet was located along the hallway leading to the transportation garage. We'd be traveling in a vehicle that from all appearances looked to be out of commission, but in reality was fueled, loaded with weapons, and waiting for us. It was genetically coded to only unlock with Elsa's, Asher's, or my DNA.

Turning the corner down the hall leading to the garage, I sighed in relief to see it empty. Maybe having a bag full of weapons along with more hidden inside the vehicle was overkill, but when faced with life or death, I'd choose being overprepared every time. I only hoped Elsa and Asher hadn't met any obstacles along their routes.

I threw open the supply closet door then hurriedly grabbed the bag hidden behind shelves back in the corner. After unzipping it, I retrieved one gun, tucked it into the waistband of my pants at my back, then strapped knife sheaths to both calves.

Before exiting the closet, I peeked into the hallway. All clear. So far, anyway. I'd breathe a sigh of relief when we were on the road to the Insurgent compound. I prayed we'd have backup from other operatives at least halfway there. For now, every precaution was warranted.

I placed my hand on the scanner beside the door leading to the transportation garage. It immediately slid open. The fact that it still worked was a good sign Silas hadn't yet learned of my transgressions. He just needed to believe in me a little longer.

Elsa emerged from the shadows in the corner to my right. Dressed from head to toe in black, she'd been nearly invisible. Only her wheat-colored hair peeking out of the beanie on her head gave her away.

"What's happening? Why did you call the abort?"

"I'll explain on the way. Just get to the SUV."

We jogged toward the back corner of the vast underground garage. The Colony owned fleets of Jeeps, vans, and luxury vehicles that spread over rows and rows. A tarp covered our SUV parked in a section of vehicles that were out of commission. Since I'd made sure a work order was never issued, it had sat quietly and untouched by the mechanics for months.

"Where's Asher?" Elsa asked.

"He should be here."

The covered SUV came into view several yards back. We were almost there. Elsa and Asher could stay hidden behind the seats while I drove us out. With me going into the field so often, no one working the gate would be suspicious. It was an everyday occurrence.

We were only three rows away when the explosion knocked both of us off our feet.

18

BRYNN

Thoughts of Ash crowded my mind as I walked into the control room. Since he'd returned to the Colony as himself instead of A36, I worried constantly about Silas discovering the ruse. Now that we had him back, a timeline for our master plan had been constructed and sent to him and Declan. We'd had no communication since then. It was too risky. Unless something went wrong, we were dark. Chess pieces were in place.

By this time, Elsa had already briefed the heads of our ally territories, and Ackerman's military connections were on alert. Anna's friends inside the Colony were ready, and Paige and I had recruited every available Insurgent sector who could reach us. Everything was falling into place. The attack on the Colony would commence in five days.

Elijah bustled from desk to desk, calling out instructions to his tech crew. They'd been working on the logistics of bringing everyone together every hour of every day since we got Ash back. Coordinating this many people in so many different areas wasn't a simple task, but the guy knew his job and would get it done.

I located Paige in the far corner of the room. If I hadn't spent so much time in and out of the field with her, I'd never suspect anything was amiss from her facial expression as she spoke to someone on her comm unit. The girl was practically a closed book and rarely gave away what was going on in that mind of hers. But even from across the room I knew from the faint tightening of her eyes and the set of her jaw that whatever she'd been discussing was serious. Trouble was coming. And it was bad.

I hurried over to her. "What is it?"

Paige held up a finger and immediately placed another call, putting it on speaker. "I need you here now."

"But I ..."

"No excuses, Noah. *Now*."

"What's happening?" I asked again.

"Declan's coming in. He's bringing Ash and Elsa with him."

My stomach flipped. It was too soon. Something had gone wrong. The plan was to meet them inside the Colony. "They're alive?"

"For now. Silas issued a kill order for Elsa. He instructed Declan to get A36 to handle the job."

I inhaled sharply. Silas must have found out what Elsa had been up to. Declan wouldn't be coming in unless he suspected his cover was also blown. Ash couldn't stay there alone. He was coming home.

"I'm not on active duty, so I don't appreciate being spoken to like that, Paige." Noah strode across the floor in our direction, his brows scrunched in annoyance. When he'd been at the top of his game pre-compound attack, my brother commanded attention every time he entered a room. Self-confidence and intelligence reflected off him like sunshine. He made things better. Resolved problems quickly and efficiently. Sadly, he hadn't been that person for a long time.

Still, I knew that man was hiding in there somewhere.

"Declan called an abort. He's coming in with Ash and Elsa. They'll need help and you know we can't reach them in time." Paige stared at Noah, her gaze unwavering. In her own way, she was pushing him to step up and become the strong Controller he'd been just months ago. "We need the inside contact. It's time to activate Aries 7."

For security reasons, throughout all the Insurgent hives only the controllers knew the identities of our informants. It lowered their risk of exposure if our operatives were captured. Technically, Paige should have received the identities of the informants when she took over for Noah, but she'd insisted the position was only temporary. She could work with them just fine in the interim without knowing their identities. Even then, she'd been confident my brother would return to the helm of this sector.

Noah eyes widened. He knew what this meant. Final lines were being drawn, and there was no crossing back. This was the end.

"They need help. Do it now," Paige urged.

Desperation iced my blood, and I turned to my brother. "Noah, you've had enough time to feel sorry for yourself over something no one blames you for. You need to live in the real world again. Ash is the closest thing to a brother you'll ever have, and Elsa was like a sister to both of us. Declan did unforgiveable damage, but even I can see he's put his life on the line to make up for it. They need you now. And so do we."

Noah held my gaze. His eyes held shadows of uncertainty, but even as I watched, strength, resolve, and confidence overrode the doubt that had haunted him these last months. He squared his shoulders, then reached into the pocket of his long leather coat and pulled out his comm unit. His fingers flew across the board. I heard the faint voice of someone on the other end as they answered. "Immediate abort. Declan, Elsa, and Ash require assistance. Maintain your cover as long as possible, and then come in with them. Insurgents en route to assist."

He turned to Elijah. "Raise Luciana and Mason. I expect their teams on the road in less than five minutes. Contact Barton and request help. We need everyone he can spare to cover Ash, Declan, Elsa, and Aries 7 until they're within our territory. We're bringing our people home alive. No excuses."

"Yes, sir," Elijah said. He spun into action and called out orders to his crew.

Our Controller was back. And so was my brother.

"Paige, put the compound on alert. We can't be sure what might be following them when they get here. Brynn, have medical on standby, then assist Paige."

Paige pulled out her comm unit and began giving orders. I looked at Noah and smirked. "I knew you were still in there."

"I won't let them down."

"I never thought you would even for a minute."

Noah gave a quick nod, then turned back toward the flurry of activity going on behind him. "Elijah, I need an update!"

19

DECLAN

The force of the explosion knocked me off my feet and sent me sailing backwards. I felt the windshield of the car I landed on crack beneath me. Stunned, I could only stare at the ceiling. Smoke rolled through the air above me. Pain splayed through the back of my head.

Somehow, we'd been discovered. Our plan was shot to hell.

Through the ringing in my ears, I heard Elsa calling my name. I rolled my head toward her voice. She grabbed the collar of my jacket and pulled me across the hood of the car. I dropped to the concrete floor beside her where we took cover between the two cars. Bullets pinged the front and other side of the vehicle, and concrete chips sprayed the air as stray shots struck the floor to our left. In my confusion, I hadn't noticed Colony soldiers shooting at us.

Elsa returned fire. I shook my head to clear it and pulled my gun from my waistband, relieved it was still in place after I'd been tossed through the air.

"How many?" I asked.

"At least ten," she yelled over the sound of gunfire. "Probably more. Hard to tell with them taking cover."

Ten of them. Without Asher we were at a severe disadvantage. Our ammo wouldn't last long. Then it would come down to trying to outrun them.

"We'll never make it to the SUV. Is there a backup plan?" Elsa asked while she alternated between shooting and taking cover.

I joined her in returning fire. "Afraid it's just the two of us, kid."

"I'm down to one clip."

I'd lost hold of the bag full of weapons and cash during the explosion. Hoping it couldn't have gone far, I dropped to my stomach and peered under the car I'd landed on. Luck was partially on my side. It was on the other side of the vehicle pinned under a car door blown off from the explosion. Elsa and I were left with just the ammo in our guns and any clips we carried.

Long story short, we were screwed.

But no matter what happened, we'd go down fighting.

I crouched beside Elsa and continued shooting. Between the two of us, we'd taken out five of the ten we'd counted, but the remaining five were slowly advancing toward us.

Elsa dropped her gun. "I'm out." She unsheathed a knife from a belt at her hip. I doubted this fight would come to close combat. Silas wanted her dead, so I was sure these soldiers had orders to shoot to kill. No doubt reinforcements were on the way. By now, I'd been added to that order. Unless he planned to torture me first, I'd face death along with Elsa here in this garage.

I took aim at a soldier who'd jumped up from cover, only to be met with an empty click. My ammo was gone, too. It was just the two of us, a few knives, and our charming personalities. But mostly mine. Elsa could be a bit prickly.

Elsa met my gaze, determination written on her face. I had to hand it to her. She wasn't a quitter.

I kneeled beside her. "Sorry we didn't make it. I knew it was a risk, but I thought we'd get further than this. Silas knew. Logan ratted you out. Sure hope Asher made it."

"At least I'm not dying in service to that murderer." Her lips curved into a smirk. "Glad we're on the same side, Declan, even if you are a tragic blob of narcissism." Despite our dire circumstances, I laughed at her comment. I always knew she liked me. Deep, deep down inside.

The lack of gunfire on our side drew the soldiers cautiously closer, and they called out instructions to each other.

Elsa pulled another knife from her belt and offered it to me. "Maybe we can at least take out a couple more."

I pulled the two from the sheaths strapped to my calves. "I brought my own." A crooked smile of approval sliced across her face, and we crouched in wait ready to meet our fate.

Screeching tires and the low rumbling of an engine echoed throughout the garage. Elsa met my gaze, her brows drawn in confusion. Reinforcements maybe? Shouts among the soldiers indicated they were just as puzzled.

I chanced a glance around the car. A black SUV screeched to a halt on the opposite side of the soldiers. The passenger door flew open, and Asher leaped out, guns blasting from both hands. Soldiers dropped in every direction. Good thing his arm had healed quicker than expected. Ten others hidden behind cars took turns popping up, but he took them out like ducks in a shooting gallery. One soldier armed only with a knife managed to creep closer. I guessed he'd also depleted his ammo and this was his last-ditch effort. He stayed low, coming up on Asher's right to catch him off guard.

Elsa called out a warning. "On your right, Ash!"

The soldier sprang up a dozen feet away and threw the knife.

Asher dropped his guns, clapped his hands together and caught the knife in midflight. He flipped it around to grasp the handle, then threw it back at the surprised soldier where it embedded up to the hilt in his throat. The exchange happened so fast I wasn't sure I'd actually witnessed it.

"I think your brother just saved our asses."

"Nice of him to show up. But if he's fighting, who's driving the SUV? Is there another player I don't know about?"

I hadn't told another soul about this plan. Only Asher, Elsa, Paige, and I were in the know. Paige said our informant would meet us at the egress point, so by process of elimination that left Aries 7. Gunfire had ceased. I thought how strange it was that the silence was almost more deafening.

Until Asher broke it. "All clear. Get in the car before more soldiers show up. Move!"

Elsa and I scrambled from where we'd taken cover and ran toward Asher, hopping over bodies strewn about the garage floor. He shouldered one of his weapons as he covered us. Elsa opened the back passenger door and flung herself in, while I dove in after her. Asher slammed the door behind me.

I immediately pushed myself into a sitting position, eager to know the identity of the driver. I blinked in disbelief.

"Get us out of here," Ash growled.

She floored the accelerator and tore through the garage, speeding toward the exit. Elsa struggled to get her seatbelt on as I fell against her when we slid around a corner.

"Jade?" I asked incredulously. "Ash, what's she doing here?" My mind whirled with questions. How long had she been keeping tabs on Silas? And how had he not figured it out?

"Jade is Aries 7. She's an Insurgent informant. One of our most trusted."

"How can you be sure? She's worked for Silas for years. She might be taking us to him right now."

"Noah confirmed it. She's one of us and in contact with him now."

Only then did I notice the comm unit in her ear. She was Silas's personal assistant. He trusted her above almost anyone. And she'd been right under his nose, feeding his secrets to Patrick, Noah, and then Paige. Invaluable information. She'd risked her life every day to help us, and her betrayal was never discovered. Until today.

"The exit gate is lowering," Jade said.

I leaned around Asher's seat for a better look. The heavy metal gate was nearly halfway down, barring our exit. We'd crash into it and the SUV would fold like an accordion.

"Maintain speed and go through it," Ash instructed. "This is one of Silas's personal vehicles and it's built like a tank. We'll make it."

Jade tightened her grip on the wheel. "I hope you're right." She squared her jaw and accelerated.

I double-checked my seatbelt and braced myself. Surely we wouldn't make it this far only to be felled by a stupid parking garage gate.

My seatbelt constricted across my chest when we crashed. Asher was right. The gate snapped in half. Part of it skidded across the windshield then over the top of the SUV. I spun around to look out the back window, where I watched it drop to the pavement. It slid several feet before coming to rest against a car. But our SUV was still moving.

Jade wrenched the steering wheel to the right, tires squealing. We slid sideways before gaining traction. She wove in and out of traffic through the streets of the Colony like she'd been doing this for years. Her reflection in the rearview mirror was full of confidence and determination, not fear that her life had been turned upside down and soldiers could kill us at any moment. And most likely would before we reached the Insurgent compound.

"Four on our tail," Asher said. He snapped a fresh clip in his gun, rolled down the window, then turned and leaned halfway out.

Elsa and I ducked as gunfire pinged against the back of the car and bulletproof windows. We had nothing to contribute since we'd run out of ammo and lost the bag containing the extra weapons.

"Get the guns from under the seats in front of you. We have more in the back," Jade called over the noise of the wind blowing through Asher's window and the blaring horns of other cars as we wove in between them. I swear, this girl could easily steal my heart.

Through the back window, I watched as Asher blew out the front passenger tire of the closest vehicle behind us. It spun around and crashed into a car parked along the street. Jade continued dodging cars in front of us and even swerved onto the sidewalk when she couldn't get around them. Pedestrians screamed and leaped to the side or dove into doorways of businesses for cover. Elsa was now hanging out her window, wind whipping through her hair as she fired at the remaining followers.

"Declan, cover while I change clips," Asher yelled.

"On it!" I released my seatbelt and rolled down my window. When Asher pulled himself in, I immediately took over. Winding through traffic at a high rate of speed while aiming at moving targets made accuracy next to impossible, but I managed to shatter a windshield and clip a soldier in the shoulder.

"Pull back!" Asher called.

I ducked inside and changed clips in my weapon.

"Two more miles then we're through the gates," Jade yelled. "Noah says Insurgent support is on the way."

"Elsa, your right! Watch your right!" Ash yelled, his voice frantic.

A Colony truck emerged from a side street and turned in behind us. Soldiers stood in the truck bed, guns aimed in our direction as they fired over the cab. Elsa's body jerked and she collapsed down against the window. She'd been hit. I reached over, grabbed the waistband of her pants, then yanked her back into the SUV. She was unconscious. Blood covered her right shoulder and streamed from her left temple. I took off my jacket to put pressure on her wound while my fingers probed her head.

"How bad?" Jade asked.

"Her head is only grazed." I rolled her over and checked the back of her shoulder, relieved to find an exit wound. "The bullet went straight through."

Asher pulled back in then spun in his seat to check on his sister. He pushed the hair gently from her forehead. "Elsa?"

"She'll be fine. Wounds are superficial." Blood seeped through Ash's shirt at his left upper arm. "You good?"

He nodded, still checking over Elsa.

"Wall of guards ahead at the gate," Jade called out. "Take cover!"

I pulled Elsa toward me and braced both of us as best as I could. No time to get seatbelts on. Through the windshield, guards formed a human barrier at the gate leading out of the Colony, weapons pointed in our direction. Taking out me, Elsa, and Jade was one thing. But Asher? By now Silas had to know A36 was no longer his property, and Ash was in control. What he didn't know was that Ash had been in control for much longer than he suspected.

"Don't slow down," Ash instructed.

"Wouldn't think of it," Jade replied, as she leaned forward and sped up even more. This would not be pretty.

When they realized we weren't going to stop, many of the guards scattered, but those who didn't break formation fired on us. Never had I been more grateful for Silas's obsessive security measures as bullets ricocheted off the windows and pinged off the front grill.

A couple bodies flipped over the hood, hit the windshield, and flew over top of our vehicle, leaving bloody red splotches behind them. Other soldiers were turned into human speed bumps as Jade mowed them down, the tires jostling over their bodies. Our collision with the gate slammed my head against Asher's headrest, then whipped me back against the seat. I gripped Elsa tighter.

We were through. Out of the Colony. I allowed myself a second of celebration before turning around to see how many vehicles trailed us. At least four followed.

"Air support won't be far behind." Asher shoved a fresh clip into his gun.

Jade turned on the wipers. Washer fluid sprayed the window as the blades smeared arcs of blood across it. "Noah has teams en route to head them off and escort us in. Barton's sector is sending four teams with heavy artillery."

Don't get me wrong, Paige was damn good at her job. After partnering in the field with her for more missions than I could remember, I had every confidence in her abilities. But knowing Noah was active again, backing us up and doing everything possible to bring us in, gave me a boost. Maybe we'd make it out of this alive, make it home. If they'd have me, that is. His tactical skills were more advanced than Colony soldiers I'd met with decades of experience. Patrick had personally trained Noah, and Patrick had gotten us out of situations where the odds of us surviving was a single digit.

Ours might have fallen into the negative range this time.

"ETA on when they'll arrive?" Ash asked.

"Take my comm unit so you can talk to Noah," Jade offered. "I need to keep ahead of those trucks." Ash leaned over and plucked it from her ear, then nestled it into his own.

I pushed Elsa to a sitting position then secured her seatbelt, careful to keep my jacket pressed to her shoulder wound. She was still unconscious, but the bleeding had slowed.

"Noah, ETA on Barton's teams?" While Ash squared things away with Noah, Jade called back to me.

"Declan, get as many guns as you can from the back. We need to be prepared in case they take out our SUV."

I climbed over the backseat, taking care not to jostle Elsa. The roads outside the Colony weren't as carefully maintained. With Jade dodging potholes, it was difficult not to land in a heap on top of the cases of weapons behind our seat and injure myself.

Occasional bullets pinged against the back window when the trucks got close enough, but I stayed as low as possible in case the window shattered. Bulletproof didn't mean impenetrable. They could only withstand so much, and the soldiers knew it. Eventually, they'd crack and shatter completely. We just needed to get to the Insurgents first, then we'd have backup.

I tossed enough weapons and ammo over the seat to hold us for a while if it came to that and crawled back into my seat. Jade must have had this SUV hidden and fully stocked in case of an emergency. That, or she was a miracle worker and pulled it together in the small amount of time between me leaving Silas's office and then meeting up with Asher. She'd never given me any reason to think she was anything other than a loyal Colony employee. Not even a whiff of suspicion she was Aries 7.

The ear-splitting screech of grinding metal sounded from the back end of the passenger side. That couldn't be good.

Ash looked to the side mirror. "The back fender covering the tire fell off. We'll lose the... "

Before he could finish his sentence, the back tire blew out. The SUV skidded to the side. Jade fought for control, struggling to prevent us from flipping. Considering our speed, it would be a miracle if we didn't. There was no way we'd be able to continue with a blown tire. I couldn't believe we'd fought so hard to make it out of the Colony only to die in a car accident.

"Hang on!" Jade yelled. She whipped the wheel to the left. Tires squealed on the pavement.

The smell of burned rubber stung my nose. I squeezed my eyes shut and said a silent prayer. The SUV spun, and my head slammed against the window. Something jabbed into my leg as we came to a grinding halt.

For just a moment, there was silence. No gunfire or yelling, no rushing of air through the windows.

I opened my eyes and took in our surroundings. We'd run off the road into a thicket of trees, and the back half of the SUV on my side was halfway wrapped around one of them. Which explained why my passenger door bent inward against my leg. The side of my head ached. When I raised a hand to it, my fingers came back bloody. Head wounds always bled the most, but I didn't think it was serious.

"Move!" Asher yelled. Jade's and Elsa's side of the vehicle was exposed to the soldiers.

I reached over to release Elsa from her seatbelt. Her cornflower blue eyes fluttered open and found mine. "Wh...?"

I shoved a gun into her hands. "Get out of the car!" Years of training kicked in, and she didn't question me. Elsa took a quick glance out the window, then scanned our supplies and assessed the situation in seconds.

The tree pinned my door shut and exiting on her side wasn't an option. Jade and Asher had already climbed through his window and crouched behind the passenger side of the SUV. Elsa crawled into the front seat and exited the same way, then dropped to the ground beside Asher. Knowing we had only seconds, I tossed out any weapons within reach then slid through the window to take cover with them.

Four Colony trucks had stopped in the middle of the road, each containing at least four soldiers. Roughly sixteen of them against four of us. We'd come this far, and I sure as hell wasn't giving up yet.

Using the SUV as a shield, we did what we could to hold off the soldiers long enough for Insurgent support to arrive. Noah may have said the ETA was only minutes away, but dozens of bullets whizzing by made minutes seem like hours. Time was running out.

Asher and Elsa shot out the tires of the wall of Colony vehicles lined across the road. When help arrived, at least they couldn't follow us. I clocked a few of the soldiers trying to break away from behind their vehicles and come around on our sides.

"Watch our flanks!" Asher had the same concern.

"Why hasn't their air support shown up?" Elsa called out.

I wondered the same thing. This fight was over when they arrived.

One tire of our vehicle was flat, but Jade was small and able to crawl under the SUV. It made her a tough target. They weren't kill shots, but the leg wounds she inflicted still took down several soldiers. Not bad for someone who spent most of her time behind a desk.

"I'm out!" she called, and I tossed another clip under the SUV to her.

"We're taking heavy fire. Update on ET... " Asher grunted as he took another hit to the shoulder. Blood sprayed the air behind him.

"Declan, on your right!" Elsa shouted.

As I spun around, a bullet whizzed close enough to my temple that I was sure it left a hairless strip. I dropped to my knee and put two rounds into the head of a soldier emerging from the thicket. When he fell, another stood behind him. Somehow, we'd missed them. I pulled the trigger, but my weapon gave an empty click. I glared at the face of the soldier who would kill me.

A halo of blood erupted from his head, and he dropped to the ground beside his comrade.

I spun around to see Elsa standing behind me. Blood dripped from the shoulder wound she'd sustained in the chase, and a new patch seeped through her right side. She'd saved my life. Pulling a gun from her waistband, she shoved it into my hands. "It's all that's left."

Jade, Elsa, and I emptied the last of our clips. Elsa dropped to the ground and leaned against a tire. She grimaced as she raised her face to the sky. Jade crawled out from under the SUV and kneeled beside her, holding pressure on the wound in Elsa's side. Sweat, dirt, and blood streaked Jade's face, but her determination was unfaltering. Even so, we were all but defeated.

Asher was down to his last few rounds and used them sparingly for the soldiers advancing toward us. They knew we were finished. At least we'd given them a good fight and cut their number by more than half. The four of us were still standing. For how much longer, I had no idea. I figured Jade, Elsa, and I had only minutes to live. Silas had probably issued orders to bring Ash back, but he would never let them take him alive.

"Damn it!" Asher tossed his empty gun to the ground and squatted beside us. "The three of you get into the trees and hide. I can handle these five. If I go down, run."

"No!" Elsa screamed, grasping his arm. "We stay together. You're not leaving me again."

Asher's shoulders slumped, and his eyes softened. "I'm not leaving you, Elsa. This time I'm saving you." Then he looked to me, his expression stoic, a silent plea in his eyes. "Declan, get them out of here."

I nodded and reached for Elsa. Ash spun around to face the soldiers inching toward us.

20

ASHER

Noah had done his best to get reinforcements here to help us, I knew that, but if I couldn't handle these last five soldiers by myself unarmed, we'd be four bloody bodies lying on the side of the road by the time they reached us. Maybe they had orders to take me alive, but that wasn't happening. Never again. At least I could give Elsa, Declan, and Jade a slim chance to get away.

Elsa wasn't having it. My little sister finally lets me know I matter to her when we may have only minutes to live.

Boots shuffled across the pavement behind me. The soldiers were closing in. With Elsa still protesting as Jade and Declan pulled her away, I bent over and picked up the empty rifle at my feet. I'd crush the skull of the first person around the corner of the SUV with the butt of it. I raised it in anticipation. They were close.

Beneath Elsa's objections and the rustle of the approaching soldiers, I picked up the faint, low rumble of engines. More soldiers or Insurgents? Didn't sound like air support. It could mean the difference between life and imminent death for us. I tilted my head and listened closer. It was coming from the south. A grin split my face. I whispered, "Thank you, brother."

"Declan, stop," I yelled. He looked at me questioningly, but I could tell when the sound of trucks reached his ears. His confusion turned to relief. "Insurgents."

The four of us ducked behind what was left of our vehicle and let our friends do their job. With only five soldiers remaining, it didn't take long. Barely a challenge. After a brief exchange of gunfire, it was over.

"Someone call for an escort?" I knew that voice. We rose from behind the SUV. Declan and Elsa limped along, her arm slung over his shoulder, his arm around her waist for support. Jade didn't appear to have suffered any gunshot wounds that I could see, but her face and arms had sustained cuts from crawling beneath our vehicle. I bled from several wounds, none of them serious. We were the walking wounded, but all things considered, it could have been a million times worse.

Luci stood on the running board of the first truck, four others blocking the road behind her. She scanned the bodies littering the highway, then took in our collective wounds and discarded weapons scattered at our feet. "Looks like we got here just in time. Damn good to see you, Ash." Her warm gaze flickered over to Elsa and Jade, then turned murderous. Luci immediately raised her weapon and pointed it at Declan. The others followed her lead. Noah hadn't told them about him.

I moved in front of Declan. "He's with us."

"He hasn't been with us in months. You *know* what he did. He's responsible for so many of our people dying. Move aside, Ash."

"I promise you he's an Insurgent. He's been working with us on the inside." I swallowed hard, hoping she'd believe me. "You'll have to get through me first, and I don't want to hurt anyone else today. Trust me, Luci." Words I never thought I'd be saying in defense of Declan.

She kept me in her sights for a few more moments, then slowly lowered her weapon and ordered the other Insurgents to do the same. "I swear if you're wrong about him I'll make sure you regret stopping me."

"I know you will."

She glared at Declan. "Let's get you guys loaded up before reinforcements arrive."

Relief settled over me like a warm blanket on a wintry day. After so many months of being separated from my family, so much time away from the person I loved most all while committing acts I hoped to never remember, the day had finally come.

I was going home.

• • • • •

Other than the general direction of south, I didn't know where our new compound was located. I only knew south because Noah had instructed Jade to drive in that direction. After Brynn was taken and our old location destroyed, I'd traveled directly from the safehouse to the Colony for what I'd thought was an exchange of my freedom for Brynn's release. It was safer for the Insurgents that way. If I didn't know, A36 couldn't give the information to Silas.

The jostling of the truck had lulled Elsa into sleep. My arm held her tucked to my side, and her head rested against my shoulder. No doubt I had a dopey grin on my face at the thought she'd finally accepted me as her brother again. Her wounds had stopped bleeding, but all four of us needed to visit medical when we arrived at the compound.

Jade had been speaking with Noah almost nonstop since we'd gotten on the transport. I marveled that she'd been in deep cover for so long and had never been discovered. For the past eight years, she'd sat feet away from Silas nearly every day listening, observing, and noting nearly everything he did and then reported it to the Insurgents. Because of her, we'd saved untold numbers of hostage lives at harvest centers. We wouldn't have made it today without her.

Declan sat across from me. His eyes were closed, but I knew he wasn't sleeping. He'd made the right call with the abort. Silas may have believed I was still A36, but once I refused to eliminate Elsa, the truth would have come out. Declan's involvement wouldn't have remained a secret for much longer.

"Thank you, Declan," I said.

His eyes shot open. "For what? Nearly getting all of us killed? For getting Jade to blow an established deep cover to rescue us?" He ran his hands through his hair, then banged his head back against the wall of the van.

"For getting my sister out of there in time. For giving all of us a chance to survive. You did the right thing."

Declan's gaze dropped to the floor. His face twisted in anguish. "If it wasn't for my own stupidity, you and Brynn would never have been held captive. The Colony wouldn't have destroyed our compound, and so many lives wouldn't have ended."

"You're right. You made a catastrophic mistake that altered the lives of a lot of people. That's something you'll have to make peace with somehow. Maybe you never will. But from where I sit, you've been trying to atone for your actions for months now."

"Yeah," he huffed. "Too little, too late."

I shrugged the shoulder Elsa wasn't leaning against. "Maybe. Maybe not. We've all done things we're not proud of. These last several months as A36 are a blank right now, but when the floodgates open, I'll probably want to throw myself off a cliff.

"The important thing is that whatever happens after this, when it's all said and done, the good you've done should outweigh the bad."

The corner of Declan's mouth turned up. "Between the two of us, that's a colossal mountain of badness we need to outweigh."

"This isn't something we can shoulder on our own. We'll have the support of friends and family to help us through it."

He huffed out a breath. "You will, Ash, but me? My roster of friends is empty. Luci's reaction made it pretty clear. I won't be welcomed back with open arms."

"For whatever it's worth, you've got me. Soon everyone will know how you helped the Insurgents by putting your life on the line for us."

From the passenger front seat, Luci turned toward me. "We're here, Ash. A lot of people are waiting for you. You ready for this?"

I couldn't hold back the smile that split my face. "More than you can imagine."

Gently, I shook Elsa awake. She protested at first, then stretched and rubbed her eyes. I was home. I'd never been here before, but for me home wasn't a physical place. My home was wherever Brynn was. And she was here.

While I hoped Jade, Elsa, and I would be welcomed by most of the Insurgents, I knew some of them would like nothing more than to kill Declan slowly and watch him suffer for what he'd done. Luci was ready to put him down the second she saw him. If I hadn't stepped in front of him, he wouldn't be sitting across from me. I'd make them understand they could trust him now. Every day he'd been behind the gates of the Colony, every second he spent with Silas, hell, every time he breathed, he'd gambled with his life. That level of constant fear took a toll on a person, but it was the least Declan felt he deserved. He'd borne that danger bravely for months.

The van rolled to a stop. Adrenaline rushed through my veins at the anticipation of who waited for me outside this vehicle. The back doors swung open. Medical personnel greeted us, and Declan and Elsa were assisted out first.

"Asher, we need to check your shoulder, so step over …"

I shoved past them in the direction of the group of people gathered behind them. My wounds could wait. I wasn't dying in the next fifteen minutes and could get patched up later.

The crowd of Insurgents parted like the sea as someone barreled through them, shoving them aside when they were slow to move out of her path.

Brynn.

At the last second before colliding with me, she leaped into the air, and I caught her as her arms wrapped around my neck. I held her tightly and buried my face into her hair, inhaling her scent. Months apart from my other half. Many of them not knowing if she was dead or alive. My external wounds were superficial, but the internal wounds were deep, jagged, and painful. Holding Brynn, knowing she still loved me, still believed in me, was the first step in healing.

Her lips met mine. Maybe we kissed for seconds, maybe it was minutes—I would have happily stayed there forever while everything else around us fell away.

Until someone cleared his throat.

"You never could keep your hands off my sister."

I reluctantly set Brynn back on her feet and pulled Noah into a hug. "Thank you, brother. We'd have never made it back without you."

"It's my fault …"

"No. Don't you ever say that. All of us made mistakes. No one is to blame. No one. You understand?"

I felt him nod. We pulled back and looked at each other.

"You look good, Ash. A little beat up, but good."

"Um, you just really don't." Dark crescents sagged beneath his eyes and his face was gaunt. Noah looked like he hadn't slept a full night since the last time I'd seen him.

He met my gaze and nodded, but the doubt I saw there said he still didn't believe what I'd said. Noah had a long history of being his own worst critic and would continue to shoulder that blame no matter what anyone said.

"My boy." Anna's voice was soft, and her eyes glistened. She pulled me down to her level so she could kiss my forehead, then searched my face. When her eyes tightened, I knew she'd seen the depth of my terror over the blank spaces in my mind. The people I'd hurt. But I knew she'd be there for me. "I prayed every day that you'd come home. I was certain you'd never stop fighting to make your way back to us."

My throat tightened, and I smiled at the woman who'd been a mother to me longer than my own. Who'd been alive to love me longer than my own.

She looked to my right. "Elsa!" Elsa moved in beside me, her eyes downcast. "I'd recognize that beautiful mass of curls anywhere. You've become a lovely young woman."

After what I'd seen Elsa do, lovely young woman wasn't the first description that sprang to mind when I thought of her. Dangerous, cunning assassin. Infuriating, overbearing sister.

Elsa had been incredibly young the last time she'd seen Anna, so I knew she was practically a stranger to her. Even so, when Anna pulled her into a hug, the worry lines in Elsa's far too young face softened, and her body gradually slumped into Anna's as if she'd finally found the support she'd been searching for. She missed a mother's touch, and Anna's hugs were the best. You felt safe and unconditionally loved in her arms, and the weight you carried was just a little lighter. I could see Elsa felt the same way.

A sudden hush came over the crowd gathered around us, but soon gasps of shock and anger filled the air as they recognized Declan.

"Traitor!"

"Murderer!"

"Go back to the Colony where you belong!"

Those were some of the nicer words called out as he stepped away from the medical personnel after being treated. Even some newer recruits who hadn't been there when our other compound was destroyed joined in. They knew his name and had clearly been informed of his betrayal.

Declan held his ground, but kept his eyes downcast, not wanting to add fuel to the unruly crowd around us that was only growing louder. Over the top of Brynn's head, I noticed three guys clustered together, their words too soft to hear. Maybe for everyone else, but I heard every word.

"...not going to stand for this. He's responsible for Jonah's death. Alex's, too. Are you two with me?"

Something had to be done or this could turn ugly fast. "Where's Paige?"

"She's already inside," said Brynn.

Declan stood with a resigned expression, ready to accept his fate which would be decided by Insurgents who were unaware of what he'd sacrificed.

"Noah, you need to say something," Brynn hissed. "Get this under control before it goes off the rails and becomes a bloodbath."

He nodded, strode over to Declan, took him by the upper arm, and pulled him through the crowd up to the top of the stairs leading into the compound. He held up his hands to hush the crowd. After a long string of more curses and threats, they reluctantly quieted down enough to listen.

"I haven't been your Controller for several months now, but Paige kept me informed of all ongoing operations. A lot of you remember Oz, an exceptional operative, someone who had your back in the field, and a guy who won the hearts of nearly every child we rescued." Noah paused and cleared his throat. "You also know him as Declan." Grumbling flowed through the Insurgents, and voices rose again in protest. "Even if you weren't with us at our old compound, you've heard stories about our losses and know he's responsible. It was the worst kind of betrayal."

Heads bobbed in agreement. Some Insurgents wiped away tears, while others cast threatening glares in Declan's direction. Still at Noah's side, he kept his gaze fixed to the ground. I leaned into Brynn and spoke softly. "Wasn't he supposed to be defending Declan?"

Noah held his hands up for silence again. "For security reasons, most of you don't know that Declan's been working for us at the Colony for the past several months. He helped my mother and sister escape. He told them about the trackers Silas had implanted in their bodies. He risked exposure every second of every day funneling information to us as he worked closely with Silas. Hundreds of hostages' lives were saved along with many lives of Insurgents, maybe even some of you, when he warned us of ambushes. He's the reason Asher, his sister Elsa, and a deep cover informant are still standing after he called an abort and helped bring them home to us."

Grumbling turned to words of astonishment. Uncertainty replaced looks of condemnation.

"How do we know all of them aren't working for the Colony and came here to kill us? A36 was there for months, and some of us saw the things he did. What proof do we have?"

I stiffened in surprise. Some of them didn't trust *me*. My own memories and actions as A36 remained cloaked in shadows, but the atrocities I'd undoubtedly committed were engraved in the minds of everyone who'd seen me. Of course Insurgents had also witnessed them. I flinched as I imagined what they might have seen. In their place I'd also harbor suspicions.

I squeezed Brynn's hand and then leaped up the steps to stand beside Declan and Noah to offer my reassurances. "I don't blame you for questioning my loyalty. When A36 is given free rein, he does what he was built to do. He kills. I know it's difficult to understand this, and I don't expect forgiveness." In my heart, I doubted I'd ever forgive myself. "While I was at the Colony, Silas demanded unspeakable atrocities of me. To make sure I carried out orders, he threatened the lives of the people I love. As Asher, I was unable to follow his commands, but I knew I had to protect my family. A36 has no qualms regarding the sanctity of life. I had no choice but to let that persona take control. I don't know everything I've done these last months, but I'll have to live with the destruction and loss of life I caused."

I clasped Declan's shoulder. "If it wasn't for Declan, I might still be out there killing for Silas. Even knowing A36 would massacre him for working against the Colony, Declan took a tremendous chance and arranged for Brynn to meet with him—with me." My gaze sought hers in the crowd. "She brought me back from the place I'd barricaded myself in my mind. Because of Declan's efforts, A36 is back under my control." I looked over the Insurgents standing before me, grateful they'd at least stayed and listened. "Forgiveness is hard, I get that. Just know that he's been working his ass off, taking precarious risks every day since he left us. At least give him a chance."

No "Welcome to the Neighborhood" gift baskets were in his future, but not everyone shared expressions of condemnation and contempt. At least they weren't coming after him with pitchforks and torches. If Declan could earn back Brynn's trust, an almost impossible feat, I was sure most of the Insurgents' opinions would sway in his favor before long.

"Thanks, Ash," Declan said, his voice low. "You speaking up for me will go a long way toward keeping all my appendages attached to my body. I appreciate it."

"Just keep showing them who you are. They'll come around."

With the full moon high in the sky now, most everyone gathered outside began entering the compound. Some probably had missions on their agenda, and others headed to their rooms to get some rest. I pulled Brynn to my chest and wrapped my arms around her. My body ached with exhaustion, nothing that a few hours of sleep wouldn't cure. But right now, sleep was the last thing on my mind. I hadn't been alone with Brynn for months.

I bent my head down and whispered in her ear. "So, where's our room?"

She tilted her chin up and looked at me, the smile I'd missed so much stretched across her face and one brow arched. "You're assuming we're sharing a room?"

I balked, suddenly doubting where we stood. Didn't she want to be with me? Had I been gone too long? Maybe it was everything A36 had done that was pushing her away. I pulled back slightly and felt my cheeks color. "Um, sorry, I just thought...we've always been in the same...I guess I can stay with Noah?" Stammering wasn't something I did often, but I was incapable of forming a complete sentence right now.

She stood on her tiptoes and pecked my lips. "Idiot. Of course I want you in my room. Our room. But that was before Mom was here. I'm not sure how she'd feel about it."

My eyes widened. Anna. It hadn't even occurred to me. Brynn and I had been on our own for so long without parental guidance, it was easy to forget we weren't technically adults. Anna had practically raised me, and I'd never do anything against her wishes or disrespect her in any way. She wasn't a fool, though. It's fair to say she didn't assume we were pure as the driven snow. We didn't hide our feelings for each other.

Standing nearby, Noah must have overheard our conversation. He slung an arm over my shoulders. "Well, this is a bit awkward, don't you think?" I wanted to smack that teasing grin right off his face. "Guess you'll be bunking with me, bro."

Brynn shrugged. "Maybe sneak in later tonight?"

I snorted. Relegated to typical teen status, sneaking into my girlfriend's bedroom at night. Sure, we were both teenagers, but typical? It wasn't a label that described any of the teen Insurgents. We were forced to grow up fast and handle adult problems and situations far sooner than we should have.

Paige poked her head outside the door. "Did you guys forget the meeting in the conference room? Let's move it." She looked at Noah and grinned. "Everyone's waiting, Controller."

He grimaced, but I could tell it was only half-hearted. He was ready to get back to work.

"I know you're all tired, but we've got some food waiting. See you in there in five." Paige let the door close behind her.

The corner of Brynn's mouth quirked up. "She's been a kick-ass Controller, Noah, but she's ready to hand over the reins to you again and get back in the field. It'll be good to see you return to the chair, big brother."

Noah raised an eyebrow. "Like you haven't been trying to force me back into it for months now?"

"Who else was going to get you to quit feeling sorry for yourself, put on your big girl panties, and get back where you belong? Just doing my job."

Noah rolled his eyes, then opened the door and entered the compound. Brynn pulled me in behind her.

A hand gently gripped my upper arm. "Asher, can I speak to you first?" Anna looked up at me.

"Of course." I turned to Brynn and brushed her lips with mine. "I'll meet you in there."

Except for a few medical people who were still packing up supplies, the area outside had been cleared. Declan and Elsa had already gone inside, so that just left Anna and me. She tiptoed up, put her arms around my neck, and hugged me close.

"I'm glad to have my children home again. I never stopped worrying about you after Brynn and I escaped." She lowered back down and took both of my hands into her own and gripped them tightly. "The three of you have been on your own for so long. Circumstances required you to grow up fast with no guidance from me or Patrick these last years. He'd be so proud to see the people you've become." Her eyes twinkled in a teasing manner, which made me wonder where this conversation was going. "I may be an old woman..."

"Anna, you'll never be old," I interrupted.

She beamed at me and continued. "If you remember, when I came to you at the Colony before we left, I told you I knew how you and Brynn felt about each other before you did. So did Patrick. Maybe it was inevitable the way you grew up together, but I see how deep your connection is. Brynn and I have had some heartfelt conversations while you've been gone. Pretty revealing talks."

Heat rose from my neck and creeped into my hairline. My face had to be every shade of red known to man. "I love Brynn more than anything. I've never taken advantage of her or her feelings for me. We..."

She placed two fingers on my lips to hush me. "Sweetheart, I know. Any fool can look at you and know your world revolves around her. It does my heart good to know someone cares for my daughter that way. Lord knows, she can be a prickly one." I chuckled. Prickly was as good a description as any for Brynn. "Without trying to make things awkward for you—"

"A little late for that now," I interrupted again.

"Room assignments don't have to change because I'm here. Just please don't make me a grandmother in the near future?"

Considering all the life-threatening, precarious, dangerous situations I'd been in, I never thought my cause of death would be embarrassment. But here it was. "Anna, I'm... we'd never..." Cue the stammering again.

"I know, sweetheart," she smiled. "Now, would you like to escort me to the conference room?"

I shook my head to clear it after such an abrupt change of gears in the conversation. "You'll have to escort me. I don't know where I'm going."

21

ASHER

A simple dinner of sandwiches and pasta salad weighted down my plate. It had been hours since my last meal. I was ravenous, and my stomach growled so loudly Brynn laughed.

"Good to see you haven't lost your appetite," she said. "Looks like Silas fed you well."

I shrugged and continued adding more food to the already heaping pile that threatened to spill over.

"Don't be a total pig, Ash," Elsa said. "Save some for the rest of us." She was falling back into the teasing sister role pretty easily. And I loved it. After believing she'd never accept me again, I was overjoyed to have any interaction with her.

Noah gave us ten minutes to wolf down dinner before starting the meeting. He'd easily donned the role of Controller again. Standing at the head of the conference table, his voice was strong, confident, and assured. But his appearance didn't match the voice. With his mocha skin tone now leaning more toward gray and the dark crescents drooping beneath his eyes, he could easily have been mistaken for a zombie.

Brynn, Declan, Paige, Elsa, Anna, Jade, and I were gathered around the table. Luciana, Mason, Barton, and a few team leaders from his sector joined us. It had been quite a while since our paths had crossed. In person, anyway. When Noah's eyes lingered on Barton as he scanned the table, I knew he was once again berating himself for not making the call to follow-up on Declan's claims. I sensed he'd always hold onto the blame no matter what anyone said.

Noah cleared his throat. "Let's get introductions out of the way. We've got a lot to discuss. Most of you are familiar with the name Aries 7, who's been a reliable, invaluable informant since my father was Controller. This," he gestured toward Jade, "is Aries 7. Jade worked as Silas's personal assistant for years and without her help, our friends wouldn't have made it out of the Colony today." How right Noah was. Declan, Elsa, and I wouldn't have escaped that parking garage on our own. Jade nodded stoically as we applauded. Noah continued around the table introducing the Insurgents Jade didn't know or had never met in person. When he got to Paige, Jade's posture stiffened, and she visibly paled. It was a strange reaction to someone I didn't think she'd ever met. She recovered quickly as Noah moved on to Barton. I glanced over at Brynn to see if she'd noticed anything, but she was in a whispered conversation with Luci. Paige looked at Jade with her head slightly tilted as if she was also puzzled by her reaction.

"I'd like to thank Barton for responding so quickly with backup from his sector. We'd expected to be inundated with Colony air support but were fortunate they never showed. Must have been our lucky day."

More like we'd won the lottery. If Colony jets had assisted with chasing us down, the four of us wouldn't be sitting here right now. The fight would have been over almost before it began, and our bodies unidentifiable mangled masses lying on the side of the road beside our crashed SUV. I couldn't imagine Silas not sending a crew after us.

"Noah," Jade said, glancing up from her data pad. "I just received an update from a Colony soldier contact. We have Colonel Ackerman to thank for air support not being deployed. Silas issued the order the second we got through the gates, and Ackerman disobeyed it. When his second in command attempted to enforce it, all hell broke loose at the control center. Gunfire was exchanged and Ackerman killed his second. Unfortunately, he was also wounded and died shortly after."

I jerked back in surprise and nearly fell out of my chair. Colonel Ackerman, the man who'd helped Everly keep Brynn and me imprisoned at the Colony, had been on our side? I'd always thought he bled for Silas and the Colony. Maybe he'd missed his calling as a covert operative.

Instead, he'd died saving four Insurgents. Taking the big picture into account, he'd also saved countless others he'd never know about.

I turned to Declan sitting beside me. "Did you know?"

He nodded slowly. "I recruited him about a couple months ago. The day I caught him trying to snipe you at the gun range."

I balked at that little tidbit of information. Ackerman had tried to kill me? As A36, no doubt I'd deserved it. Still, I took back every bad thing I'd said about him. He'd given his life for us. "What else haven't you told me, Declan?"

"Prepare yourself. I couldn't tell you everything. And you're welcome for convincing him not to shoot you."

Noah nodded. "The Colonel hadn't been with us for long, but his efforts made a big impact in this fight, and we thank him." He bowed his head a moment as if offering up a silent prayer. I added my own message of thanks, wherever he was. Raising his gaze again Noah asked, "Where does that leave us with the Colony soldiers he recruited and the military from the other territories?"

"His backup is Major Daniel Cortez," Declan replied. "Ackerman was a smart strategist and planned for a scenario like this in case something happened to him. He ordered Cortez not to break cover and to proceed with the original plan. He'll contact the military leaders in the other territories. They'll remain on standby until they receive word from Cortez."

A lot of planning and strategizing had taken place while I wasn't around, and with all this talk of allies I felt seriously out of the loop. Kind of in an entirely different orbit. "You guys have been busy," I whispered to Brynn.

"You're not the only one who can save the day," she smirked and squeezed my hand under the table.

Noah continued. "Okay. We've had some unexpected developments happen today. We hadn't planned for this, but we're prepared. Our timeline has moved up. The original plan called for us to infiltrate the Colony in five days. We can't afford to wait that long. Right now, Silas's energy will be directed toward locating Jade, Asher, Elsa, and Declan. This level of betrayal won't stand. He'll appear weak and incompetent to both his friends and enemies if he doesn't take immediate action to retaliate. With all the allies we've gathered the Colony will be dismantled. It's just a matter of getting all parties involved to activate sooner than we originally intended. We've never had an advantage like this, and we're not losing it on my watch." He looked at Elsa. "Are Adria, Grales, and Baithe ready?"

She nodded. "They're also on standby and ready to engage."

Wait—what? What's happening? I looked at my sister in disbelief. "Silas had you kill Flores and Kimathi. How is it you're working with their territories?"

"I never killed them. Silas only thought I did. I'd been searching for an opportunity to find allies for months. When he ordered me to take out Flores, his wife, and children, I knew it was the opening I'd been waiting for. The same with Kimathi. I might have appeared to be his good little assassin, but that was part of my strategy." Her face softened. "I haven't forgotten the values our parents instilled in us, Ash. They just fell to the wayside for a bit."

I swiveled to Declan beside me. "And you never told me?"

He rolled his eyes. "If I'd let you know everything Elsa was doing, you'd have made some big Asher gesture to try and protect her. You can't save everyone. We both know she's perfectly capable of taking care of herself. Besides, the fewer people who knew the better."

I looked back to Elsa. "So, all this time you were plotting against Silas and didn't tell me? I could have helped you."

"Can you blame me for not trusting you? I hadn't seen you for a decade and didn't know who you were anymore."

"Ash," Noah interrupted, "Can we put a hold on the family drama and move on to more important matters? As Declan said, you can't save everyone, and Elsa did a damn fine job without you."

I shot a look of anger in Elsa's direction. She shrugged me off and focused her attention on Noah. "Sorry, Noah." I slouched in my chair and crossed my arms. Yes, I was sulking. Elsa was too young to be caught up in something so dangerous. I shuddered to think what might have happened to her if something had gone wrong. If Silas had found out. Which was exactly what happened today. What if he'd never confided in Declan, I'd still been A36, and Silas ordered me to terminate her? Would A36 have done it?

Brynn leaned over and spoke softly. "I know it's against every instinct you're feeling for Elsa, but you can't be so overprotective of her. You'll just push her away. She's not a little girl anymore. It took a lot of intelligence and bravery to do what Elsa did, and you should be proud of her."

I exhaled loudly. Everything she said was right. Deep down I knew it, but it was going to take some time for me to adapt to the role of big brother again without stepping on Elsa's toes.

My issues needed to be put on the backburner for now. Noah needed my full attention because clearly I needed to catch up on what was happening. As he went over the details and timelines for the many moving parts of our attack, I understood what he'd meant about us never having these kinds of advantages in the past. If everything went as planned, the Colony could be destroyed. Plenty of things could go wrong. Every mission came with risks, but it sounded like Noah and Paige accounted for those risks and developed contingency plans.

"Are there questions?" Noah asked, looking around the table. The room was silent. "No? Good. We leave at 0200 tomorrow. Rest while you can."

• • •

Finally, the strategy meeting was over. I gave medical ten minutes to remove the bullets from my left shoulder and sew me up, then Brynn and I practically raced out of there as she led me down hallways and past other Insurgents who called out greetings. I raised a hand in response, but if anyone tried to stop me they'd be shoved aside. My mind was entirely focused on being alone with Brynn after months apart.

The walk was endless. How many hallways were in this place? Kind of like that mirage of seeing a door at the end of a corridor, but the closer you got, the further it was. After what seemed like miles, Brynn stopped in front of a worn wooden door and then pushed it open. I slammed it closed behind us just in time for Brynn to shove me against it. Her lips were on mine, but it wasn't a gentle kiss. It was hard and demanding with months of pent-up fear, anger, need, and hunger fueling us. This was the first time I'd felt whole and content in months, and I surrendered myself to her. To us.

An hour later we lay on our bed with Brynn's head resting on my chest and my arms around her, our legs entangled. "I missed you so much," she said. She curved her body in closer to mine as she ran her fingers over the necklace my father had given me. I'd worn it for years without knowing about the chip he'd hidden inside that revealed the secret of my creation. "I never gave up hope that you'd come home. I just didn't know how long I'd have to wait."

I tightened my arms around her and pressed my lips to her head. "You're the last image I had when I surrendered to A36 and the first thing I saw when I came back."

"You don't remember seeing me at the hostage facility?"

My brow furrowed, and I pulled back to see her face. "You ran into A36 during a rescue?"

"He unexpectedly interrupted our mission. You were supposed to be at another facility, but for whatever reason decided to come to the one we were infiltrating. A36 and I had an interesting exchange."

My stomach sank. I was almost afraid to ask the question. "Did I hurt anyone?" I swallowed hard, hit by a sudden realization. "Did I hurt you?" I whispered.

"Only minor injuries to the team. Mason might have cursed your name a few times while he limped around for a month." She cupped my cheek. "And no, you didn't hurt me. I always said you never could, and I was right. You told me to run."

Relief crashed over me like a wave, and my head fell back to the pillow. I didn't remember that night, but at least I'd had the presence of mind to warn her away from me. Despite my apprehension, Brynn had always remained adamant that I'd never harm her. And A36 hadn't. "You always believed in me more than I did myself."

"And I always will. No matter what. Unconditional love right here," she said, pointing to her heart.

She was unaware that her faith in me had been like a life preserver to a drowning man. Even when I'd thought I'd never see her again, knowing someone like Brynn could love me the way she did made me believe I was a good person. Despite the things I'd done. A dark shadow crept into my thoughts. What about the things I was unaware I'd done? My body tensed in sudden fear.

Brynn felt the change and raised up on an elbow.

"Tell me what you're thinking."

"What happens when I remember everything? All the horrible things I did as A36. I keep waiting for the dam to burst, and the memories of every person I hurt, threatened, tortured, or killed will flood my brain. How can I live with that, Brynn?"

She cupped my cheek and looked down at me. "We'll deal with that when it's time. I'll be with you every step of the way, and we'll work through it. You're surrounded by people who will support you. After tomorrow, the healing can begin."

In her mahogany-colored eyes I saw nothing but determination and love. I wondered if I'd ever stop dreading the day I'd see loathing and disappointment.

"I'll need all the support I can get. Once we put the Colony behind us, I've got some dark days ahead of me."

"And I'll be right here."

I stared at the beautiful smile she saved only for me and pushed two long braids over her shoulder. "I'll never figure out why you're with a guy like me, but I'm so grateful for you, Brynn Wallace."

This time when I kissed her it was tender and soft. Then I pulled her close and held her against me for the remainder of the night, praying this wasn't the last we'd spend together.

22

ASHER

I bolted across the roof of the building in the direction of the sniper stretched out on his stomach. With the cacophony of gunfire and shouts below, he couldn't hear my approach. Leaping onto his back, I brought my hands to either side of his head and then snapped his neck. Declan and Elsa were on the ground six stories below across the street. One of them had been the sniper's target, whose finger had been poised to pull the trigger.

Declan's and Elsa's accurately placed shots had just taken out two more guards on the street level. They hadn't seen the sniper I'd disposed of.

From the vantage point of the roof, I monitored ongoing battles below and sniped Colony soldiers where I could. Smoke rose in the distance from a burning building, and the bodies of soldiers and some civilians who'd fought back littered the streets. Regrettably, the bodies of Insurgents and allies joined them. Most of the citizens had barricaded themselves in their homes once we'd breached the gates, and we'd encouraged them to stay put. We had no quarrel with them as long as they stayed out of the way.

The battle was still ongoing and had been long, bloody, and grueling, but I refused to think about the number of people I'd killed over the past several hours. I was a weapon doing what weapons did best. Feeling any guilt only left room for errors. Declan said I couldn't save everyone, but I could sure as hell try.

Along with our allies from the territories of Adria, Grales, and Baithe, we'd stormed the gates of the Colony in the wee hours of the morning. Grales and Baithe had also provided air support and taken out Silas's fleet before they'd gotten airborne. Knowing we'd strike soon, the soldiers had been prepared for us, but our numbers overwhelmed them. It was clear Silas hadn't known about the other territories joining us in battle. Most of what was left of the Colony's defenses had pulled back to form a barrier around Silas's tower, the place where I'd resided against my will for over half a year. From our inside contacts, we knew Silas was holed up there, probably in his safe room.

"Ash, proceed with your team to the Tower," Noah instructed over my comm unit.

"On it."

Since Declan, Paige, Elsa, and I were familiar with the layout of the Tower, we were the obvious choices to infiltrate the building. The four of us also had personal reasons for wanting to be present at Silas's final curtain call. It would be a show we wouldn't want to miss.

"We're moving in," I relayed to my team. "Luci, what's it look like your way?"

"We'll clear a path for you. Be careful, Ash."

Luci's team was ahead of us, working their way toward the direction of the Tower. Knowing Brynn was with Luci's team gave me an extra boost of confidence. Her team was well-equipped with experienced and talented Insurgents I trusted. Mason's team waited outside the Tower and, along with our allies, had already significantly reduced the barricade numbers. A twinge of hope fluttered in my stomach. This could all end today. But I tamped it down. Call me superstitious, overcautious, whatever you'd like, but we still had a turbulent ride ahead of us and a long way to go before I could think about celebrations.

Still, what a joyous party it would be.

I rushed down the stairwell to meet my team at street level. They'd taken cover in an alley while waiting for me. Plenty of our comrades had fallen, and the four of us weren't unscathed. We'd all suffered injuries, more added to those we'd received yesterday during the escape, but thankfully they were minor. With her sleeve, Paige wiped a trickle of blood from a cut on her forehead. Elsa pushed sweaty hair away from her dirt-smeared face. She favored her right leg and must have twisted her ankle because I saw no signs of a wound. Declan used his teeth and free hand to tighten a tourniquet around his left upper arm where a bullet had grazed it. I'd sustained two gunshot wounds to my right shoulder and a deep knife cut on my left forearm, but all were in various stages of healing already. The bullets would have to be removed later.

"This is the final stretch. Everyone ready?" I asked.

"Ready to witness the fall of Silas?" A sly grin spread across Declan's face. "I can't wait. Let's take this party to him."

Paige and Elsa nodded, as eager as Declan and I were to finish this.

"Noah, we're advancing," I said into my comm unit.

"Luci, Mason—are your teams in place?" he asked.

"Ready, Noah," Mason replied.

Gunfire and shouting rang out ahead of us from the direction of the Tower where Luci's team was. My heart stuttered when she didn't answer. Brynn was with them. Three other sets of worry-filled eyes stared back at me, but Paige raised her hand in a stopping motion and shook her head, telling me not to panic. Give Luci time to reply.

"Luci, respond," Noah ordered. His voice was level, but I heard the undercurrent of fear running beneath his words. He was just as worried.

A crackle filled my ear, then I heard Brynn's voice. "Luci's down. I'm leading. We've got you covered, Ash."

Brynn's words were a punch to the gut. Paige, Declan, and I had worked with Luci on so many missions I'd lost count. Elsa had only known her for hours. Luci's team had brought us home just yesterday after we'd escaped the Colony.

"Not Luci," Declan said, shaking his head in sorrow. I knew what he was feeling. Her death was a personal loss that stung all of us, but we'd properly mourn her and many others later. We had a mission to finish. Our most important one.

"Right now, Luci would yell at us about wasting time," Paige said. "We need to go."

I nodded in agreement and shouldered my rifle. "Let's move."

With only five blocks standing between us and the Tower, the four of us moved swiftly, dodging bodies lying in our path. Seeing the previously pristine tree-lined sidewalks in this state was almost surreal. Unattended vehicles blocked the streets after being abandoned by citizens who'd run for shelter when we'd breached the gates. We jumped over glass fragments on the pavement from broken windows and storefronts. This avenue bore no resemblance of Silas's utopia. His false utopia.

As we drew closer to the Tower, where the remaining soldiers had fallen back to protect Silas, a higher number of dead littered the street. Avoiding the blood that pooled beneath their bodies wasn't an option. In some spots, there was so much it ran into the storm drains. We'd known Silas would have a deep barrier surrounding him. It would have been easy for our air support to just take out the entire building, but there were still innocent people inside who had never killed anyone. The young operatives were also there. Some of Ackerman's people had ensured they were sheltered from the line of fire and unable to join in defense of the Colony. I doubted many of them would if given the opportunity.

I didn't immediately see any soldiers around the entrance to the Tower, but appearances could be deceiving. Occasional shots rang out, but they were in the distance. Still, you never knew who might be sniping from the top of a building or a high window. While Declan covered our six, I led us across the courtyard toward the entrance. Insurgent and ally teams spread out around us to flank the building. I did a double take when I saw the statue of Silas in the center of the massive fountain, which now spewed red water. A few bodies lay draped across the rim, but others floated atop the blood-tinged surface.

We entered the front doors. Our footsteps on the white marble floor echoed inside the two-story lobby. Afternoon sunlight drifted in through overhead skylights. Every desk, sofa, and chair sat abandoned. It would have been eerily silent, but soft music still played in the background from hidden speakers. We came to a stop. Getting inside had been easy, but I didn't know the status on the upper levels. There could be more soldiers waiting for us.

I activated my comm unit. "Are we clear inside the Tower?"

"It's Cortez, Ash." I recognized Major Daniel Cortez's voice, Ackerman's backup. He and his soldiers were already stationed inside the Tower when the attack began. They'd been instrumental in shutting down any internal defenses and keeping tabs on Silas. "We've swept the building. You're clear up to the top floor. Silas barricaded himself inside his office and has an unknown number of soldiers guarding him. We're holding the floor until your team arrives. Elevators are shut down from the tenth floor up."

"ETA ten minutes, Cortez."

"Copy that."

"Silas will go for his panic room," Declan said.

Elsa nodded. "He's too much of a coward to face us. Instead of surrendering, he'll let all those soldiers die protecting him."

"You expected anything less?" Paige asked. "What a homecoming this will be. Don't you just love surprises?" She grinned in anticipation.

Until just hours earlier, only Declan had known about Paige being Silas's daughter. It came as a shock to the rest of us but explained why she'd been so driven and worked tirelessly as an Insurgent. I understood her deep-seated need to try and compensate for all her father's sins, and there had been many. Knowing it was an impossible task to outweigh them, she'd still done everything in her power to save people.

"The panic room won't be a problem."

"Ash, you know it's blast-proof, bullet-proof, and every kind of proof there is. How do you plan to get him out?" asked Declan.

I raised a brow and smirked at him. "Trust me. It's not a problem. Enhanced genes, remember?"

Declan rolled his eyes and muttered something about enhanced arrogance. I ignored him.

"I sure wish flying was in your skillset, so we didn't have to climb twenty flights of stairs," Elsa said, wincing.

"Got it covered," Declan said. "Ash may be a superhero, but I was a top dog in the Tower. I know the codes to get the elevator up and running again."

Elsa cast a doubtful look at him. "Wouldn't your clearance be canceled after the way you bugged out of here? Silas isn't stupid enough to overlook something like that."

Declan shook his head in disappointment and sighed. "You underestimate me as usual, Elsa. I might have kind of glanced at Silas's code and memorized it. Also Ackerman's. And possibly Jade's. A guy's gotta be prepared."

He hadn't been lying. One of the security codes worked but I didn't know whose. All I cared about was getting to the top floor sooner. It had been a long night, and we were all grateful to not have to expend extra energy trudging up several flights of stairs. I'd alerted Cortez that it was us on the elevator and to hold their fire. When the doors opened at the penthouse level, he was waiting to greet us.

"We could have proceeded into Silas's office but wanted to wait for you. I understand this mission is of a personal nature for your team. More Colony soldiers are inside, some I undoubtedly know, but I'd prefer not to face off with any more of my friends today if possible. We have an alternate way of infiltrating the office if you're amenable."

"I'm amenable to just about anything, as long as it gets us inside those doors," I said.

Cortez's plan would spare the lives of soldiers, and I liked the sound of that. Let them be incarcerated when this was all over instead of dying to protect someone as unworthy as Silas.

Both teams took cover as one of Cortez's soldiers kicked open the door, then dove to the side. Shots rang out from inside Silas's office, but their defense would end shortly. Canisters laced with a fast-acting knockout agent were tossed through the open doorway.

The guards inside shouted in confusion as the gas erupted. We heard bodies fall to the floor, but soldiers stopped a few as they escaped into the lobby where we waited. Cortez and another man, both outfitted with gas masks, entered the office. Glass shattered when they shot out one of the floor-to-ceiling windows to air out the room.

"Clear!"

We entered Silas's office. Eight bodies lay unconscious on the floor, their weapons lying beside them. Cortez's soldiers carried them out as the four of us gathered around the gray stone wall that hid Silas's panic room. The sole entrance was cleverly built into the stones so that if you didn't know the door was there, it was easy to miss. I imagined Silas hunkered down inside, knowing his time was short, that all his defenses had failed. I wondered if he was sorry or even regretted anything he'd done. Knowing his inflated ego, I doubted it. He'd never seen all people as equal and never would. His hierarchy included him at the top, citizens of the Colony next, and everyone else fell into the levels beneath them.

"He can hear you, and there's a camera hidden above the door," Declan said, pointing to a small hole in the ceiling I hadn't noticed.

I looked up, certain he watched me from behind the door sniveling in fear. I waved in greeting and flashed him A36's best dangerous smile.

"You can make this easy by opening the door and surrendering, Silas. Or not. You created me and know what I'm capable of. That door won't keep me out. There's no question I'll drag you from that room, it's just a matter of how soon. What's it gonna be?" His silence was all the answer I needed.

"What can we do to help?" Elsa asked.

"Stand back."

When Silas had believed Declan was one of his sheep, he'd proudly shown him the safe room. Even bragged about it but stated it would never be used for its intended purpose. Colony security was unbreachable. The room was overkill. He'd truly believed no one could defeat him. The Colony would always stand. Declan pointed out the nearly invisible seams outlining the door in the stone.

High on Silas's wish list of my enhanced qualities had been strength, athletic ability, and endurance. Given his overwhelming hubris, I doubted he'd ever imagined I'd use these abilities against him. This was the perfect opportunity to make him regret that oversight. I landed a stepping side kick against the wall. Shards of stone crumbled to the floor. Clouds of rock dust floated on air drifting in through the broken window. After a couple more skillfully placed kicks, the dust became thicker, causing Paige to sneeze. One more kick cracked the remaining stones and sent them tumbling to the black marble floor in pieces.

Elsa clapped in admiration. "Nice job, big brother."

I'd exposed the panic room door. An image of Silas cowering behind it curved my lips into a smile. I hoped fear gnawed at his cold, black heart and slowly devoured him from the inside out. He deserved to feel one thousand times the pain of every hostage he was responsible for killing.

The outer layer of the door was smooth silver that was now scratched from the destruction of the stones. Declan was probably correct in saying it was bullet-proof, blast-proof, and every other proof invented. Getting through wouldn't be the easiest thing I'd ever attempted. But I enjoyed a challenge.

I closed my eyes and thought about all those months away from Brynn, what Everly had done to her when Brynn was imprisoned here, how Silas had threatened my family and forced me to commit unthinkable actions to keep them safe. A dark rage simmered deep inside me. I fed it with visions of children being taken from their families and led to harvest facilities. The flames grew higher. Silas's plans to use my offspring to create an army. A roar clawed its way up my throat as angry fire exploded within me. I spun and channeled all that energy and fury into a powerful back kick that left a sizeable dent in the door.

Declan's eyes widened in amazement. "Nice, Ash! Way to use those powers for good. Remind me to thank you later for not using that particular move on me while we were in the sparring ring."

My kick might not have penetrated the door, but it had buckled enough that it pulled away from the frame. Just wide enough to slide my fingers through.

"Be ready. When this door comes off, Silas will be armed. We're not letting him out of this office. Understood?" I asked.

"Him getting away was never an option," Paige said. "This is the end."

Declan and Elsa nodded in agreement.

I inched my fingers into the gap beside the doorframe. When I had a solid grasp on it, I pulled, gradually increasing the pressure. The metal screeched in protest from the duress, but I didn't let up, still not having given it my full power. Applying more pressure, the metal reluctantly gave and moved toward me. All it needed was one good yank to fully open. A quick glance over my shoulder reassured me Declan, Elsa, and Paige had taken cover. If the door went flying across the room, they wouldn't be injured.

Summoning my strength reserves, I imagined it flowing through my arms and shoulders. Despite what I'd told Declan, I needed every ounce I possessed to gain access to this panic room. I grasped the edges of the door again and tugged it outward, pouring everything I had into the effort. The reinforced door gave a long, final groan as it wrenched free.

I raised it over my head then heaved it to the side. The marble floor beneath it cracked and splintered. Bullets pinged off the metal doorframe as I rushed into the panic room. Silas had always been a poor shot. He'd never had to defend himself. Maybe he should have spent more time on the gun range than looking in the mirror.

The panic room was as opulent as his office to ensure Silas was comfortable during his self-imposed imprisonment. Leather sofas, expensive tile, shelves of books, and a bed topped with a white silk comforter and piles of fluffy pillows. Even artwork adorned the walls. Excessive and utterly ridiculous.

He stood directly in front of me behind a fully stocked bar, glass shelves loaded with a wide variety of liquor extending to the ceiling. A bourbon glass sat nearly empty on the counter beside him. Every time I'd seen Silas, his appearance was immaculate. Not a hair out of place. The man before me was falling apart. His tailored suit was disheveled, and his hair stuck out unevenly in every direction where he'd run his fingers through it. His trembling hands held a gun trained on me.

"I'm not leaving this room." His voice quivered as much as his hands.

"You can walk out, or I'll drag you out. Make your choice." My voice was flat and unemotional. I was ready to end this.

He narrowed his eyes and squared his jaw. I knew he'd take another shot. I lunged across the bar toward him as he pulled the trigger. The shot went wide. My body crashed into his, the momentum carrying both of us into the glass shelves behind the bar. Liquor bottles exploded as they toppled to the tile below. Glass shards littered the floor, and the robust smell of alcohol surrounded me. I rolled away from him, untangled my limbs from his, grabbed the gun where it had fallen beside him, then tossed it into the corner.

Silas moaned and blinked in confusion, dazed from our collision.

I kicked him over onto his stomach, and he yelped in pain. Gripping the back of his collar, I jerked him up then dragged him across the floor toward his office. He struggled to grab onto furniture or anything else he could get his hands on to slow my progress, but it was useless. I dropped him in a whimpering, foul-smelling heap in front of his desk. Paige, Declan, and Elsa stood across the room by the conference table in a semi-circle, their expressions jubilant even as they trained their guns on him.

In two entirely divergent ways, Silas had created Paige and me. He'd added and deleted parts that were unacceptable in his distorted image of perfection. With Elsa, he'd tried to mold her into what he'd hoped Paige would become, but Elsa had been strong enough to hold onto the values and beliefs our parents had instilled in her for more than a decade after they'd died. In a macabre, disturbing way, Silas was a father to all three of us. He'd surrounded himself with beauty, fantasized about and created it nearly his entire life. The three of us were vital pieces of his utopian dream, but it was a nightmare that had held us captive in different, painful ways.

I believed the odds would be in my favor if I bet patricide was on all three of our minds right now. It was at the forefront of mine. No doubt Declan would join in.

Silas groaned as he rolled over, pushed himself into a sitting position, then leaned against one of the supporting columns of his desk.

"It's over, Silas," I said. "The Colony has fallen."

He dragged his gaze up to me. Even with his wrinkled, ripped suit and his unkept hair full of glistening glass fragments from the liquor bottles, his expression was full of arrogance and disbelief.

Was he delusional? Didn't he understand what was happening?

"You might have made it through the gates and somehow gotten past my incompetent guards, but it's only a matter of time before our ally territories arrive. The four of you and every other worthless Insurgent won't live to see tomorrow. The Colony will prevail."

Declan stepped forward. "You have no allies, Silas. Grales and Baithe joined in the fight with us. All the neighboring territories stand with the Insurgents. You're done."

Silas balked in shock and looked as if he'd been slapped. All these years, he'd believed himself untouchable behind his gates. Other territories had known about gene stripping and all the heinous acts that went along with it. Silas provided them with operatives and assassins to take care of their internal problems, so they'd looked the other way. Until Silas had come for them when they didn't fall into line as he'd expected.

"You have me to thank for that," Elsa said, as Silas's gaze darted to her, his face full of venom. "Once I shared your plan for the leaders and some of their families to meet their end in unfortunate accidents, they were eager to join us. In your overzealous need for power, you made a severe miscalculation that resulted in a victory for us."

Silas fumed as he listened to Elsa. He'd been betrayed by the two people closest to him. "I practically raised you," he spat. "I provided you with a home and everything you wanted. Because of me you're no longer that clumsy, pathetic child who clung to her siblings. You have me to thank for turning you into a strong, independent young woman. And what do I get in return? Lies, betrayal, and treachery. You conspired against me. You're nothing but a worthless disappointment."

"I never asked you for anything. I was a scared little girl torn away from everything familiar and everyone I loved. Because of you, I lost my family.

You turned me into a killer. But you taught me one valuable lesson, Silas." Elsa's mouth curved into a smirk. "You taught me to play the player, not the game. And that's exactly what I did to you."

He screamed in rage and started to rise from his sitting position on the floor.

I shoved him back down. "You're not going anywhere." I said.

His chest heaved in anger, gaze darting around the room as if searching for an exit. Then he froze as his gaze fell on Paige, who'd stepped forward out of the shadowed corner of the conference area. His mouth dropped open in shock.

"Sabine? Is that you?" His voice was soft and almost reverent. This was the first time he'd laid eyes on his daughter in years. He'd probably presumed her dead. A genuine smile broke over his face. It was convincing enough to make me believe he'd actually missed her. "You've finally come home."

Paige straightened, her head held high. "That's not my name anymore. I'm not that person, and this isn't my home."

Her words had an effect on him. Hurt flashed across his face and he drew back. "You're with them?"

"Since the day I left." Paige's tone was calm, but firm. Knowing his own daughter rejected his beliefs, had walked away and worked to undermine everything he'd done, must have felt like an ice pick to his heart.

I hoped the shards pierced every corner of his body.

"I told you I'd never recognize you as my father again. You made choices for me without my consent, decisions that required other people to die. Where were their choices? They were adults and children snatched from their families and loved ones for the vanity of everyone in the Colony. What gave you the right to end their lives?" Paige paused and swallowed hard. She'd held tightly to these feelings for years, never sharing her secret. Until last night, none of us knew what she'd gone through. Every harvest facility we raided was a reminder of the cruelties her own father was responsible for. Every child she rescued and spent time with before they were taken to safe houses was alone and frightened because of Silas. Finally having this moment to express those feelings to him had to be cathartic for her. "I won't apologize for not being good enough for you. The fault is yours, not mine. You never loved me. You don't possess the emotional capacity to love anyone other than yourself. I was just a prop to complete your skewed picture of the perfect family."

Silas looked as if the world had been jerked out from beneath his feet. Sad, even. In his own contorted way, I think he cared about Paige. Maybe even envisioned the day she'd return home and they'd be a family again. Even monsters had dreams. Now his were destroyed. The Colony had fallen, those closest to Silas had abandoned him, and the pedestal he'd placed himself on all those years ago had toppled from beneath him. His kingdom had collapsed.

"It's time to go, Silas." He ignored me and leaned against the desk, legs sprawled in front of him, head hung down. "I can make your trek downstairs very uncomfortable. Get up."

Everything happened fast. Silas jerked his head up. Hatred burned in his eyes. I leaned over to grab his arm, but he sprang from the floor before I reached him. He swung his arm away from me, pointing a gun toward the next closest person.

Where the hell had he gotten a gun?

I didn't have time to think. Saving Paige, Declan, and Elsa was my only goal.

A shot rang out as I lunged toward Silas. A body dropped to the floor behind me.

Elsa screamed, "Declan!"

I crashed into Silas. He shouted and futilely struggled against me. I drove him back toward the wall of windows. We hit it then went through it. Blood exploded from the back of his head from the force of the impact. Glass shattered around us, and then we were falling.

I guess Declan was right when he said I couldn't save everyone. I just hoped I'd saved them.

EPILOGUE

I didn't die, although the pain I experienced on waking two days later almost made me wish I had. My fall was only ten stories, a height that would kill most people. Not me and my enhanced healing genes. I landed on the roof of the wing that housed the young operatives.

Silas wasn't so lucky. He fell the full twenty stories, screams ripping from his lungs the whole way down. He landed in the fountain in the courtyard at the front of the Tower, the one spewing red-tinged water from the blood of soldiers who'd fought in his defense. Another few feet and I would have shared that fountain with him. In the seconds before I hit, I shoved him away from me. That momentum was enough that he missed the ten-story drop. His fate would probably have been the same, but I couldn't take the chance.

Enhanced genes or not, a ten-story fall still caused plenty of damage. I'd broken a considerable number of bones in my body—many I'd never heard of—and sustained some severe cuts on my face both from crashing through the window and when I hit the roof. My shattered bones pieced themselves back together, but it wasn't without bouts of excruciating pain. Brynn had barely left my bedside for the two weeks I was laid up. Once I was coherent and she knew I'd survive, she wasted no time in telling me she was ready to kill me for what I'd put her through. Couldn't blame her for that.

Despite being a crap shot, Silas's bullet had hit Declan. It was a chest wound, but he'd recovered. Silas's weapon had come from one of his soldiers felled by the knockout gas. When Cortez's people had carried them out, they'd overlooked a gun that had fallen to the wayside and had been missed during all the commotion. It was sheer, dumb luck Silas had managed to lay his hands on it.

Brynn delivered the disturbing news, with a teasing smile no less, that Elsa had divided her time between my bedside and Declan's. I'm still turning that one over in my mind and trying my best not to be the overprotective big brother. No one will ever be good enough for my sister no matter who they are, but if Brynn can accept Declan after everything that's happened, that's a huge point in his favor.

Noah kept me updated about what was going on with the territories and the fallout of the Colony collapsing. Although still a work in progress and far from over, there had been serious discussions about uniting the territories under one elected leader. It sounded like a move in the right direction.

Harvest centers that had been the site of thousands of killings were dismantled. Citizens had left flowers, candles, pictures, and stuffed animals in honor and remembrance of the hostages who'd been executed. For me, they were reminders of all those we couldn't save.

This was my first day out of the Colony's hospital. The scientists and doctors here were better equipped to deal with my injuries and so long as none of them tried to kill me or experiment on me, Anna had given consent for treatment since I'd been unconscious for those first few days. She'd also brought me meals she'd made herself, proclaiming the hospital food to be subpar. I was thankful every day she was back with Brynn and Noah and was here to mother me.

Brynn's hand was in mine as she led me down a hallway inside the Tower. It seemed strange to freely walk the corridors here without anyone chasing us. I still felt the urge to peek around corners or take cover behind something. Getting over that feeling might take quite a while.

"Can you at least give me a hint where we're going?"

She rolled her eyes. "I already told you it was a surprise, so quit asking."

It soon became clear she was leading me toward the young operatives' wing—the roof I'd landed on and the location where I'd first been reunited with Elsa. I couldn't help remembering the hurtful words she'd spat at me that day. I knew her feelings had changed and that she loved me as her brother, but unlike my physical wounds, the emotional one was slow to heal. But we had time now that our war was over. Time to learn how to be a family again.

I'd been correct about where Brynn was taking me. Sure enough, she stopped in front of the double doors leading to that area. I frowned. "This isn't a place I want to revisit. I don't need any more reminders of what happened here."

Brynn cupped my cheek and smiled. "Get ready to replace those bad memories with some wonderful new ones."

She turned and pushed open the double doors. My eyes widened in shock. I stood dumbfounded. Inside was a hive of activity. The enormous common living space had been subdivided into offices and a reception area. People filled every available chair, their attention focused on data pads. Several gathered around the multitude of overhead monitors that displayed pictures of adults and children. I walked over to the window that overlooked the expansive training area below where I'd first seen Elsa. What was formerly a place where teens learned to kill and maim was now a playground with groups of children running about and playing. A smile split my face at how carefree and happy they were, the threat of being captured by Colony soldiers now behind them.

I turned to Brynn. "What is this place?"

"Come with me."

She guided me behind the bustling reception area into the largest office. Paige sat behind a desk working on a computer. She looked up when we entered and rose from her chair, coming to greet us. Paige had never been the touchy-feely type, but the smile on her face and sparkle in her eyes said enough. She was relieved to see me standing.

"They finally released you. You look good for someone who broke over half the bones in his body." She chuckled.

I glanced around the room. Bright sunlight shone through the windows onto a comfortable seating area. In the corner was a play section with an overflowing toybox, piles of stuffed animals, and a shelf filled with children's books. I looked back at her in question. "You work here? Behind a desk?"

Paige gave me a teasing grin. "Glad to see that fall didn't damage your comprehension skills, Ash." She looked around the room with pride. "This is my office. There's not much demand for Insurgents these days, so I had to get a new career. And it's my dream job. The monitors you saw in the lobby are pictures of adults and children rescued from harvest centers. All those people on their data pads in the waiting area are leaving their contact information and the names of their missing loved ones. We're reuniting families."

I'd never seen Paige like this. She glowed with happiness. She'd always spent time with the children we'd rescued from harvest centers, reading to them and playing with them before they were transported to safe houses. Helping to bring families back together was truly her calling. She'd found her life's purpose, and it thrilled me.

"How are you doing this? This project must cost tons of money to run."

"Well, Silas did one good thing for me. He must have expected me to come back one day. That or he just forgot to change his will." She held her hands out to either side. "All of this is mine. I'm his only living beneficiary. All his blood money will be put toward helping to rectify the pain he caused, whether it's reuniting families, helping them find homes or jobs, or just get back on their feet. I don't want any of it for myself."

Her words struck me momentarily speechless. It had never occurred to me what might happen to Silas's assets when he was gone. That he would have something as ordinary as a will. "You said we?" I asked when I found my voice again.

Paige tucked a strand of hair behind her ear and pointed to a door on her right. "Declan and I have adjoining offices. We started this project together."

I stood silently for a few beats and blinked. In one way, this was the last thing I'd expected and yet—it was perfect. They both loved children, and finding their families or placing them with new ones was a natural fit. "You and Declan?"

Paige shrugged. "I know, right? We work well together, and our goals are the same. Finding homes for kids is our priority. We've talked, and his feelings for me are nothing more than friendship. Besides, I'm pretty sure he's got his sights set on someone else. And I think she feels the same way."

I scowled. "I've heard." Brynn tried to repress her laughter, but it bubbled out. It had been so long since I'd seen her this light and carefree, and I'd never grow tired of it.

"I've got some other news. Pretty shocking news, actually," Paige said.

"Not sure if I can take much more. This morning's been filled with surprises already."

Paige's expression softened. Had she also found someone? "I've learned I have some other family. Well, kind of like family."

My eyes widened in trepidation. Silas had more children? Extended family? What if they leaned more toward Silas than Paige? This war might not be over.

Calm down, I told myself. Paige wasn't panicking, so this must be a good thing. I backed it down a few notches. Getting used to a normal life might take longer than I'd imagined. Brynn must have felt me stiffen because she squeezed my hand reassuringly.

"I'd noticed Jade had a strange reaction to me when we met in person," Paige said. "I wondered if it had something to do with me being Silas's daughter and her working with him for so long. Turns out it wasn't that at all. Jade lost a younger sister, Mei, to genetic harvesting many years ago. It's why she set out to infiltrate the Colony and become an informant. Turns out, I'm the spitting image of Mei. Records confirmed I received her genes when Silas had me altered. It's a weird, melancholy, all kinds of awkward situation, but we're working our way through it. Neither of us has any family left, so maybe it's fate that brought us together. Families don't always have to be blood relatives, right, Ash?"

I smiled at her warmly, my heart overflowing with happiness for Paige. She deserved this and so much more. Technically, I'd never had blood relatives. Even my parents and sisters were found family. I'd always miss Mom, Dad, and Cami, and not a day went by that I didn't think of them, but I was so grateful for my other found family. Brynn, Anna, Noah, and friends like Paige who were closer to family. "They sure don't. Families can be made up of anyone you choose."

• • • •

We'd just finished the memorial service for the Insurgents and allies who'd fallen during the attack on our compound and the final battle at the Colony. A marble wall had been erected with the names of those we'd lost. After the ceremony, Brynn and I had lingered to look for the names of the Insurgents we'd known personally—Luci, Jonah, and Alex. There were so many more, but those three were operatives we'd worked closely with. Especially Luci. I missed her.

Declan had attended with Elsa, their hands entwined. Not everyone was thrilled to see him there, but he had my respect. It took an enormous amount of bravery to show up knowing many of these deaths resulted from information he'd handed over to the Colony.

The day I'd been released from the hospital, I'd seen Declan and Elsa sitting at an outdoor table finishing lunch. Elsa rose then headed back indoors. I saw the wistful gleam in Declan's eye as she walked away. I knew that look from personal experience. With Elsa gone for the moment, I grabbed the opportunity to address whatever this was between them and have a chat.

"Declan," I said as I approached the table.

He jerked his head up in surprise, startled to see me.

"Ash, um... I," he stuttered, his gaze flicking between me and the direction Elsa had gone.

"Don't even think about it."

A red hue rose from his collar and creeped up toward his hairline. "I'd never... Well, I wouldn't say never, but..."

I wanted to keep up the threatening big brother guise, but Declan continued to stammer, clearly uncomfortable. I decided to put him out of his misery.

Taking Elsa's seat across from him, I held up a hand for him to stop. "Brynn told me about you two."

He slumped back in his chair, gaze fixed on the empty plate in front of him. "I'm sorry. I'll stay away from her. It's just—"

"I'm not telling you to stay away."

His head snapped up. "You're not?"

"No. I can't say I'm thrilled about the two of you together, but I'd say that about anyone with Elsa." I studied him for a few beats. His eyes were bright with excitement, but they still held a note of caution and a hint of fear. Good. His fear of me would keep him in line. For a while, anyway. After all, it was Declan. "You've come a long way. Mistakes were made, but I'm certainly not one to judge considering what I've done. I believe you're a good person, and this thing you're doing with Paige... you're trying to do something with your life. I admire that."

He sagged in relief. "Thanks, Ash. That means a lot coming—"

"But if you ever hurt her, I'll kill you."

His eyes widened in panic.

I could seriously have so much fun with this and really wanted to continue. Instead, I flashed him a disarming smile. "Kidding. Not that you need it, but you have my blessing. Just don't tell Elsa I said that because I'll get a long lecture followed by the silent treatment. I wanted you to know I'm okay with you two."

We spent a few more minutes discussing other plans he and Paige were making. When I got up to leave, I ran into Noah only ten feet away. He leaned against a large sidewalk planter, its tree shading him from the sun beaming overhead. A teasing smirk adorned his face, and his eyes twinkled in amusement.

"You heard the entire conversation, didn't you?"

He nodded. "Welcome to my world, brother. If it were me, I would have threatened him a little longer."

"I bet you're loving this, seeing the tables turned on me."

"Guy shows up making moves on your sister, thinking he's good enough for her, and all you can do is stand back and watch." He chuckled and swung an arm around my shoulder. "But sometimes, Ash, it turns out for the best."

Smiling at the memory of Noah's words, I returned to the present. I ran my hand once more over Luci's name, then took Brynn's hand and turned back toward the Tower. We still had a lot of work ahead of us, both personally and as a community. Paige had paid for the best therapists to be brought in for anyone who felt they needed the support, and I'd already attended several sessions. Anna assisted with the young operatives who'd worked for Silas. Most of them didn't remember a time before the Colony, and they needed a tremendous amount of help from her and the therapists in transitioning to a normal life.

I still had nightmares about Silas's terrifying plan to create an army of my offspring. I didn't remember donating any... samples, but my memory was spotty at best. Silas had mentioned nothing to Declan about the project moving forward, but that didn't mean he hadn't begun. To ease our minds, teams had scoured every lab in search of any evidence the project had been started. I breathed an enormous sigh of relief when nothing was located.

Staying in the Tower was only temporary. Many Insurgents still needed to find permanent places to live, myself and Brynn included. We couldn't live in an abandoned school forever. I didn't know what the future held in store for me. Maybe I'd regain my memories as A36 or maybe those months would always be a blank. Whatever the case, I knew Brynn would be there with me, and I'd take things one day at a time while helping the community wherever I could.

It was time to move forward with the process of healing and living.

ACKNOWLEDGEMENTS

I'm a lifelong, voracious reader, and I hate ending a book on a cliffhanger, unable to learn the fates of the characters I've become so invested in until the sequel releases. To all the readers who waited over two years for this book, I apologize. It's certainly not the timeframe I'd hoped for, but a worldwide pandemic put a damper on writing, and the characters didn't want to talk. We grew tired and annoyed with each other—me with them taking so long to share the rest of their story, and them with me for taking so long to write it.

My editor, Staci Troilo, always strengthens my writing. She makes me appear to be at least a semi-educated person.

Thanks to book club friends and beta readers extraordinaire Jo Anna Young and Deanna Jenkins. Your comments and suggestions helped catch my errors and better shape this novel.

Although she's not a big fan of sci-fi or dystopian books and movies, Susan Thomison is always ready to listen and let me bounce ideas off her. Thanks for always being there.

To all the book bloggers out there, your tireless hours of reading, writing reviews, and talking about books is deeply appreciated.

A big thanks to my crafty friend Bonnie for making my book event table look so snazzy.

Thanks to Lynne for always helping with publicity and telling readers about my books.

Thanks to Reagan and the team at Black Rose Writing for everything you do. Seriously, I don't think you guys ever sleep.

As always, thanks to my parents and sister for telling anyone who will listen about my books.

Mike, Tanner, and Reese—you're the best decisions I've ever made. Most of the time. There's still the occasional day you make my hit list.

ABOUT THE AUTHOR

Teri Polen reads and watches horror, sci-fi, and fantasy. *The Walking Dead*, *Harry Potter*, and anything Marvel-related is likely to cause fangirl delirium. She lives in Bowling Green, KY with her husband and black cat. Her first novel, Sarah, a YA horror/thriller, was a horror finalist in the 2017 Next Generation Indie Book Awards.

Visit her online at www.teripolen.com.

NOTE FROM THE AUTHOR

Word-of-mouth is crucial for any author to succeed. If you enjoyed *The Insurgent*, please leave a review online—anywhere you are able. Even if it's just a sentence or two. It would make all the difference and would be very much appreciated.

Thanks!
Teri Polen

We hope you enjoyed reading this title from:

BLACK ROSE writing™

Subscribe to our mailing list – *The Rosevine* – and receive **FREE** books, daily deals, and stay current with news about upcoming releases and our hottest authors. Scan the QR code below to sign up.

Already a subscriber? Please accept a sincere thank you for being a fan of Black Rose Writing authors.